MIXED UP
LOVE

N A T A S H A
M A D I S O N

Cover Design: Alyssa Garcia Uplifting Designs
Interior Design CP Smith
Editing done by Jenny Sims Editing4Indies
Proofing Julie Deaton by Deaton Author Services

DEDICATION

Madison Maniacs, my secret place, thank you for being on this journey with me!

MIXED UP
LOVE

Chapter One

Hunter

Beep, beep. The car alerts me that I just locked the doors as I climb up the five stairs to our office, Watch Over Me Security. For almost six years now, Anthony and I have been business partners, but instead of renting office space, we decided it would be better to have our own house.

Entering the code on the lock, I open the door, noting the heat in the air. We have turned this three-bedroom house into our own office that fits our needs. Anthony and I each have our own office, and the third bedroom is shared with our crew—Dominic, Brian, and Dante.

Walking in, I'm not surprised to see Rachel, our office manager, already here. Rachel has been here from the beginning with Anthony and me. Besides being the receptionist, she is the planner and also the best tech person I've ever met, which means I can't fire her.

"Morning," she says. Her shoulder-length blond hair curled to perfection, her black rimmed glasses hiding her crystal blue eyes, she's standing there in a tight black pencil skirt that hits just past the knees and a white button-down silk shirt tucked in. Although we don't have a uniform, we usually wear black and white. Her pink stilettos give the only pop of color on her outfit. "I just put the coffeepot on," she tells me, walking toward the door, heading to the basement.

The basement is really her domain or, as she calls it, her playground. Little computer screens fill all four walls, displaying every single traffic camera we have access to—not that the city knows. Another reason I can't fire her.

I walk to my office and dump my keys and wallet, then shrug my suit jacket off and roll up my sleeves. Grabbing a water bottle, I head down to the basement. The lights are on, and Rachel sits in the middle of the room with her earpiece in. Her desk is U-shaped with four computer screens sitting on it. "Anthony is on his way," she tells me as she types away. You can never sneak up on her. I'm convinced she has this whole place wired and booby-trapped. "All assignments are accounted for." She looks up. "I need your expense report, or I may have to shoot your accountant if she calls me one more time." She smiles, and I'm not so sure she's joking.

"Hey," Anthony says, walking into the room. His huge six-foot-five frame is enough to scare anyone; that and he wears his black hair in a Mohawk of sorts. He, too, is wearing black pants and a white button-down shirt. "I brought some doughnuts," he says, grabbing a chair and sitting on one side of the desk. "I think I'm dehydrated," he says, finishing a bottle of water in a matter of seconds.

Anthony and I go way, way back—to Navy training. Of course, back then, he was a six-foot-five, one-hundred-and-fifty-pound body in a little boy. It's crazy what deployment can do for you. He hit the weights hard, and his frame filled out dramatically. We did two tours together, but after seeing so much death and escaping it many times, we knew we were done. Luckily, we got the best recommendation from our drill sergeant, and we were thrown into government detailing. Slowly but surely, we started building clientele. One politician visiting for the weekend turned into his friend giving us a call, which led to some of Hollywood's biggest names. Watch Over Me was born, and we haven't looked back once.

"You are probably dehydrated because you were up all night spilling your bodily fluid elsewhere," Rachel says, looking up with a smirk as Anthony glares at her.

"Are you keeping track of me?" he says, leaning back in his chair. "Do you have a tracker on my phone?" He now sits up and grabs his phone.

Rachel breathes out while Anthony types on his phone. "Your Fitbit is synced on my computer. You really need to slow down on round three and four." She taps her finger on her desk.

"Privacy." Anthony points at her. "Confidential."

Rachel doesn't answer. She just rolls her eyes. "One of these days, your dick is going to fall off." He gasps in fear when she says that, cupping himself. "And Tinder is going to crash!"

He slaps his hand down on the table. "Don't you fuck with my Tinder app again."

"Again?" I ask, grabbing my own chair and sitting down. "Should I even ask?"

"No!" Anthony yells, looking at her.

"What? She was cute," Rachel counters.

"She was a fucking dude." He raises his voice and then looks at me. "We didn't do anything."

"That isn't what her," she says, shaking her head, "sorry, his messages said the next day."

"I'm changing all my passwords." He grabs his doughnut and takes a bite while Rachel laughs.

"Is this where the party is at?" Dominic asks when he walks in. He's the oldest of the bunch in his late thirties. Dominic has been with us for a little over three years. We needed extra men when the Secret Service contacted us about the president staying down here for a week. He stands six-foot-six and is lean, so lean his body fat is probably zero. His black hair is buzzed on the sides and longer on top, but he styles it to the side.

"Who bought the doughnuts?" Brian asks right behind him, walking to an empty chair. Brian is smaller than the three of us; he and Dante both stand at six-foot-two.

"Why are you dressed like you're going to the beach?" Anthony asks Brian.

"Because I am going to the fucking beach," he says, glaring at Rachel from the side. "Fucking Kardashian is going to Turks and—"

"Not Kardashian," Rachel says, "Jenner."

"Does it matter?" he says, and I look at his outfit. He's wearing beige khakis with a white short-sleeved polo.

"Well, at least you won't need sunscreen," Dominic says. When we all look at him in question, he replies, "He's Asian."

"And?" Rachel says, looking up from her keyboard.

"Well, they don't sunburn. Have you ever seen an Asian man with a sunburn?"

"No," Brian says, "because we wear fucking sunscreen." He shakes his head. "Dumbass."

"Where is Dante?" I ask, looking at my watch. It's almost nine, when everyone is supposed to be in for the Friday morning meetings.

"He just pulled up," Rachel says, flicking one of the screens to the front door where we watch Dante's six-foot-two frame ducking a bit when he walks in the door. His black hair perfectly coiffed and cut short on the sides and long on the top. His green eyes covered by his aviator sunglasses. He doesn't bother going any farther into the house and comes right down the steps.

"Right on time," he says, smiling and showing off his perfect teeth. He's our pretty boy as we call him.

"You're ten seconds late," Rachel says, eyeing him and looking at the screen.

"I stepped into the door at eight fifty-nine and forty-seven seconds," he says, and I watch Rachel.

"I beg to differ," she says. "I can pull up photo evidence, if you'd like."

"Okay, you two," I say, "let's get on with the show." I pick up the pile of yellow folders. "Looks like we have the quietest weekend ever. Or next couple of weekends, for that matter."

"Except for me," Brian says, glaring, and everyone else is laughing.

"We have three state senators coming next week to play a round of golf." I look at them. "Anthony, Dante, and I will cover that."

"Brian, you have another celebrity coming to town," I say, and he groans. "It's a guy. He's coming here for a three-day vacation. Chances are he won't need you, but you're on call just in case."

"Dante, you are in the office next week," I tell him, and he just nods his head. "Next month is huge. We have the biggest music festival coming to town." This time, everyone groans.

"Great, twenty-one-year-olds vomiting everywhere," Dante says. "So glamourous."

"Remember when that girl threw up on your new Gucci shoes?" Anthony laughs, pointing at Dante. "I thought you were going to cry." We all laugh as he gives us the finger.

"I had those shoes for three days," he says. "Three."

"Well, next time, go with Adidas or Nike," Rachel says, shrugging her shoulder.

"Okay, I think that is all. I want everyone to study

the golf course, just in case we need to swap in. Also, I want to go over the layout of the music festival," I tell them. "Let's reconvene in two hours," I say, looking at the time. "Rachel, you can get lunch in since it will most likely be an all-afternoon thing."

She nods her head. "I'm ordering from Marcos, so everyone get their order to me, or I will order what I think you should eat." The boys waste no time grabbing their phones and texting her their order. The last time she did that, she ordered us all quinoa and kale salad with figs. It was so horrible. I had twigs in my teeth.

I walk up the stairs to my office in one of the bedrooms. It's a plain office with a desk, chair, and a loveseat. Pictures are hanging around the room of some of our clients, thanks to Rachel. I sit down and start studying the lay of the land for the meeting in two hours. I make some notes and draw out some exit routes.

By the time we get back downstairs, we have everything set up. I grab a copy to look over tonight, saying goodbye to everyone, then walk back upstairs. Going to my desk, I slap the files on it.

"Hunter, your mother is on line one." I hear Rachel say from the phone speaker. I'm about to tell her to take a message when she adds, "I told her you were out of town."

"Thank you," I tell her, opening my emails.

"Don't thank me," she starts. "I expect my Starbucks on Monday." I don't bother answering because I know she's already disconnected.

Opening the file again, I'm about to start making

another plan of action when I hear a knock on my door.

"I need to ask you for a favor." I look up from my computer at Anthony.

He stands there, leaning against the doorjamb. With his arms folded over his chest, the material of his shirt looks like it's about to split open. He spends a ridiculous amount of time in the gym.

"I just did you a favor last week when that country singer came to town unexpectedly to surprise her boyfriend, and we had to smuggle her in a box," I tell him, leaning back in my chair.

"That wasn't really for me," he says, thinking of a certain celebrity who was in town. "She's back in the dating game, and the paps followed her here." He smiles. "She just wanted to hang with her guy. Putting her in that crate was genius. No one even picked up on that one."

I shake my head. "I've done some pretty crazy things in my life, but putting the country's golden girl in a crate had to be one of them."

"Good times." He smiles, making me roll my eyes. It was not what I considered a good time.

"Now what do you need?" I ask him, crossing my own arms over my chest.

"I need you to pretend you're me," he says, looking at me, and I glare at him. Forget the fact he's two inches taller than I am, and where he is hulk, I'm lean. My hair is blond, cut short on the sides, longer on the top, and my eyes are gray instead of brown.

8

"How in the hell are we going to pass that off?" I ask him, confused. "Clearly, we are like day and night. Me being the day part."

"I have a blind date tonight, and well, I also have a real date tonight." He wiggles his eyebrows, and I groan internally.

"Who would fix you up on a blind date?" I ask, laughing. "You have commitment issues."

Now, it's Anthony who glares at me. "I don't have commitment issues. I just like Tinder more than I like a relationship right now." He holds up his hands. "I can't be tied down."

"You know you can get carpal tunnel from swiping right and left." I smirk at him as he just glares.

"I will have you know that the girl I'm going on a date tonight with is someone who I met through Tinder, *yesterday,*" he tells me all proud, "which means two dates, two different days, same girl. If that doesn't scream I can change, I don't know what will."

"Oh, wow," I say, throwing up my hands in the air. "Back-to-back dates." I shake my head. "Why don't you just go out with this blind date, and then go out on the next one?"

"Can't do it," he says, shaking his head. "We have an appointment at five."

"It's four," I tell him, looking at the time in the corner of the computer screen. "And what date has an appointment time?"

"Well," he says, pushing himself off the door, "I booked us the suite at the Ritz."

"Oh my god," I say, slapping my hands on top of the desk while laughing. "She's a hooker? Do you pay her at the end?"

"She isn't a hooker. She just lives with a roommate, and well, I don't know her well enough to have her come to my place," he says, coming into my office now. "Will you take my place?"

"What if she saw a picture of you from the person who set you guys up?" I counter.

"No. I already asked my mother, and she said that all she told her mother was that I was single and had a steady job," he says. "Besides, just say I cut my hair."

"Your mother set you up on a blind date?" I chuckle. "Why would she do that?" I ask him. "This is ridiculous. Just call and cancel."

"I can't. I promised my mother she could set me up once a year, and this is the day," he says. "Can you please, please just do this for me?"

"Why don't I just go and say you had an emergency?" I counter. "I can tell her that you were called away on a top-secret mission and will call her when you get back."

He shakes his head. "No because then my mother will set it up again. Please, Hunter, just do this one thing for me."

I lean forward on my elbows. "I hate liars and lying. You know this, right?" I ask, raising my eyebrows.

"Stop being so fucking noble and just go on the date. Besides, when was the last time you actually dated a woman?" he asks me.

"I think …" I stop talking, trying to think back.

Jesus, when was the last time I had a date? I point at him. "What if she falls for my charm and wants another date?"

His head tips back, and he roars out with laughter. "You? Last week, the girl at Starbucks gave you your coffee with her number on it, and you threw it out without taking a sip." He shakes his head while he continues to laugh. "You didn't even walk out and do it in secret. You did it right in front of her."

"I was letting her know I wasn't interested in her," I tell him. "I didn't see the need to beat around the bush."

"Oh, she got the memo all right." He shakes his head. "No beating around the bush with you."

"I have a bad feeling about this," I tell him, getting up and going to look out the window.

"You have a bad feeling about everything," Anthony says, going to the door, then turning back to look at me. "I'll forward you the address to meet her."

"I can't believe I'm doing this," I say under my breath.

"Oh, and try to be a human." He laughs. "Don't just grunt. Use your words."

"I have two words for you right now," I tell him as he walks down the hall to his own office. "It's one meal. How bad could it be?" I say to myself when I look down and see where I have to meet this woman after my phone beeps with Anthony's text.

Ivy Garden
6:00 p.m. reservations are under Anthony.
Her name is Laney, and she has long blondish hair.

I owe you one.

I close my eyes and count to ten, and then continue my work till it's time to go.

Chapter Two

Laney

"Mom, you have to stop doing this," I tell my mother over the phone while I scroll through my patient list for Monday. To say I was looking forward to Saturday is an understatement. I turned off my alarm this morning, and it was nice to know I didn't have to be anywhere tomorrow. I sit back in my office chair and look around. My diplomas are hanging on the wall right on top of the little couch that I bought so I could put my feet up when I have a few minutes. It's been three years, and the only time I've sat in it has been to change my shoes.

When I graduated from dental school, I knew I wanted my own practice. Slowly, but ever so surely, I opened my business with one chair and no receptionist. My mother came in and set up the office and helped put ads everywhere. The hours were long, and they were tough, but bit by bit, I grew by word of mouth, and I now had such a successful practice with five other dentists working for me.

"You haven't been on a date since Trevor broke up with you, and that was over two years ago," she says softly, and I think back to the day he broke up with me, or better yet, the day I walked out on him, and he didn't chase me. I guess surprising him at work wasn't a surprise for just him.

The office was so quiet, but it was normal since it was after hours. He sent me a text, telling me that he had to stay late to finish his latest merger deal. That was happening a lot lately, so being the best girlfriend in the world, I picked up his favorite Thai food and made my way over, but what I got was something I couldn't ever erase, no matter how much bleach I use.

I cracked the door open slowly, trying not to drop the food and the drinks I was carrying. To say we were both surprised was an understatement because he was balls deep, as they say, in his assistant, Fredrick.

My shriek startled us both, and the Thai food I was holding fell out of my hands, exploding on my favorite pair of Tory Burch flip-flops followed by the two drinks I was holding in my other hand. My hand flew to my face where I covered my eyes. When I heard the rustling of clothes being put on and the sound of zippers, I opened my eyes again. The tears pooled in my eyes as my heart was slowly shattering to little shards.

"Laney." I heard him say and then finally focused on them. They were both dressed from the waist down, but the picture of Fredrick bent over his desk replayed in

my head. This answered all my questions—why sex was always so blah, why he never really went down on me, why he was more interested in his skin care products than the fact I was sitting naked in front of him.

"You're gay?" I asked the ridiculous question. "I mean, obviously." I pointed at them, and he still said nothing.

I shrugged and raised both my hands, expecting him to answer, but all he did say was, "Um, um, um."

"How long?" I asked the stupid question. "I mean, we've been dating for four years. Four." I looked around to see if there was somewhere I could maybe sit. My heart was beating faster and faster, making it feel like I just ran in a marathon.

"We've been together for seven years," Fredrick finally said, and I whipped my head to him.

"Seven years!" I yelled or shrieked. Either way, I was pretty sure that my head was like one of those cartoons on television where the steam was coming out of my ears as I shook it side to side before it exploded. "Why the fuck are you dating me then?" I yelled, throwing my hands up.

"My parents would never approve," he finally said softly, "so I figured ..."

"It's two thousand eighteen." My voice was still loud and still shrieking. "How could anyone not approve?" I shook my head, closing my eyes.

"You know how Mom is," Trevor said. "She is all about appearances so ..."

"So, you dated me to shut her up?" I put my hand

on my chest. "How far were you going to go with this? Would you have married me?" I shook my head, pushing the tears back. No fucking way would I shed a tear in front of him. I then asked him the question that held the little bit of what was left of my heart intact. "Were you going to have kids with me?"

"I figured we would get married and have kids, and everyone would be none the wiser," he said, looking at me. He took a step forward, but the sound of Fredrick stopped him from coming to me.

"Marry her?" Fredrick looked over at him, putting his hands on his hips. "You were going to marry her?" He sounded upset as if he was the one who just walked in on his boyfriend plowing his assistant.

"Hey," I said, pointing at him, "you don't get a say in this. You're the other woman, or man," I said and looked back at Trevor. "So, you were okay with my whole life being a lie?" I shook my head. "I can't," I said, turning around when I started to feel the tingle of tears coming. The squish of the Thai noodles echoing in the room. I started to walk away, confused and in a daze.

"Laney, wait." I heard Trevor call out and turned to look at him, not even sure I knew what I was waiting for. "Will you tell anyone?"

I shook my head and looked at the ceiling. "You're an asshole."

The last words I ever spoke to him. I got into my car and drove home to my condo. The drive back to my place was a blur. I tossed my shoes in the trash and walked up the cement stairs to my door. I undressed and took a hot shower, scalding almost, then when I came out, there was a text from Trevor's sister. I don't know why I was expecting maybe a couple of missed calls from him or a text message, anything, but instead, I got the shittiest text of my life.

I'm sorry it didn't work out. We love you.

I tossed my phone on the bed and groaned.

I spent the night mourning my relationship, and then the next day, I swore off men. I mean, I wasn't jumping ship, but I was just not going to rush it. Well, now, here I am two years later, and my mother is setting me up on a blind date. It got so bad that she had to set me up.

"You know he's engaged, right?" My mother's voice breaks me out of my daydream, or day nightmare.

"Who is?" I ask the question even though I'm afraid of the answer. My neck gets hot, and my hands get clammy. I open my Facebook, going straight to Trevor's sister, Nikki, and right there in the middle of her Facebook profile is a picture of my douchebag closet gay ex-boyfriend Trevor and a blonde smiling at the camera, holding her finger out to show off the ring. "Oh my god," I say, whispering out loud while I read the caption. "We couldn't be happier. Congrats, Trevor and Cassy." *How is this happening?* I ask myself. "I can't believe this."

"I know, honey," my mother says softly. "It must be a shock."

"You have no idea, Mom," I tell her. I close my eyes, and shaking my head, I make a decision I might regret but what the hell. "Send me the information about the blind date," I tell her as I hear her squeal and clap her hands.

"You won't be sorry," she says and hangs up.

"Oh, this can go both ways," I say to myself. I inhale and exhale as my phone pings with a text.

Ivy Garden

6:00 p.m.

His name is Anthony, reservation is under his name also!

You won't regret this and have fun.

"I'm already regretting this," I say to myself as I turn and look out the window. "What's the worst that can happen?" It's a loaded question, I know, but I'm thinking it can't get worse than it already is, right?

Chapter Three

Laney

"Can you believe he's engaged?" I say to my best friend, Sandy, as I walk up the steps to my condo on the beach.

"What I can't believe is that you never told anyone that he swings for the other team," she says as I hear a horn honk in the distance. "You could have called his stuck-up mother and said 'lady, my 'gina is missing a piece.'" I laugh. Sandy and I have been best friends since her family moved next door to mine when we were both eight years old.

I spotted the big moving truck while I was in the living room, running to the kitchen and telling my mom that people were next door. We both watched out the window as they unloaded the truck, and when I finally saw the pink bed, I knew there was a girl next door. I gathered up my Barbie dolls and packed them in their plastic bag and made the trek over. It was friendship at first sight. It also helped that we were the only girls on the block and the only children in our family.

When we were thirteen, we camped out in the backyard on our first night of summer break, and there, under the moonlight, we stabbed our index fingers and became blood sisters. We did everything together—we even lost our virginity at the same time but in different rooms. We went to college together, we moved back home together, and now, we lived right next door to each other. We were also opposites. I'm blond with long hair, and she has a black pixie cut. I don't have one tattoo on my body, and she's covered from her neck down.

"Can you imagine? She would have probably shit herself," I say and then hear another honk. "Where are you?"

"I'm on my way to my date," she says, and I laugh. Another thing we are opposite about—I date, and she doesn't.

"You don't date, you Tinder," I tell her, and she laughs.

"Don't hate the player," she sings, "hate the game."

"They have a word for women like you; it's called a man-eater."

"Oh, please, I will have you know that this is the second date with the same guy," she says, proud of herself. "The same guy back to back."

"Really?" I ask, shocked. She doesn't do repeats. Ever.

"Yup," she says, and I picture her sitting in her car with a huge grin on her face.

"So, you're bringing him home?" I ask, holding the phone with my shoulder as I put my key in the door. I open the door to my condo and walk in.

"Whoa," she says, "relax there, butterfly. No, he got us a room at the Ritz."

"Baller status," I tell her, and she laughs. "He might even make it rain."

"You are trying so hard to be cool." I laugh, knowing it's the truth.

"So why did you decide to go on a second date with him?" I ask, kicking my shoes off at the door, then bending to pick them up and carry them back to my room. My unmade king-size bed sits in the middle. I have about eight down-filled pillows all over my bed, and the sheets were the most expensive things I've bought, but it was one thing I didn't bend on.

"One, he's gorgeous; two, he is built like an ox; and three, it's hands down the best sex I have ever had in my life. And I've had a lot of it," she says. "Like a lot a lot."

"Oh, he sounds like a keeper," I tease her.

"Bite your tongue," she says. "I gotta go. I just got here. If I end up dead, his nickname is Mohawk!" She disconnects before I can tell her to be careful. I walk out of my bedroom and open the door to the patio. Stepping outside, I allow the sound of the waves hitting the shore to get me back to my happy place.

I walk to the railing and look over at the beach where families are packing their stuff to head home. I turn to sit on the plush oversized couch underneath my awning. Curling my feet under me, I people watch for about thirty minutes, then get up and go inside to change from my scrubs.

Walking back into the house, I toss my scrubs into the laundry basket in the corner of my closet and then walk into the adjoining en suite bathroom. The gray tiles feel cool on my feet as I walk past my white two sink vanity and lean into the glass shower to turn on the water. I wish I had more time because I would have taken a nice bath in the deep tub that sits on the side of the shower. I shower quickly and then walk to my closet, heading straight to my summer dresses. After the dreary news, I need to wear something that makes me smile. Grabbing my blue short summer dress, I step into it, bringing it up, and then tying it behind my neck. The halter dress leaves my shoulders and arms bare. The elastic at the waist brings it in and makes it flow around my legs. I grab a white belt and also some pearl bracelets. Sliding on my tan wedges, I grab my small champagne Coach purse and pick up my keys and sunglasses on my way out. I arrive at the restaurant five minutes before six, the Uber dropping me off in the parking lot right to the side of the Ivy, so I walk around the brick corner to the front door. I pass the outdoor patio made to look as if you are sitting in a garden. Black cast iron tables with matching chairs sit on white cement blocks. Hanging from the awning are vines with white and orange roses on it. It looks magical.

Walking into the restaurant, the hostess stands there with a smile on her face while I look around and see if maybe there is a guy sitting alone. I notice a couple of guys at the bar, but they look like they are together. Most of the tables are taken but none of them with a single man. "Good evening. How many I help you?" she says.

"I'm supposed to be meeting someone, and I don't see him, reservations under Anthony," I say, still looking around. The clanking of plates and cutlery fill the room along with soft music coming out of the speaker. She looks down at the pad in front of her.

"Yes, Anthony, table for two?" she asks, and I look at her and nod. She grabs two menus and another one that I'm assuming is the wine list. "If you can follow me," she says and walks to the right of the restaurant. Passing a couple of tables, she sits me at a table for two near the bar and in front of the outdoor patio. "Here you go. Your waiter will be right with you." I take the seat facing the front door so I can see everyone coming in and out. I grab the linen napkin on the table under my utensils and place it on my lap. I grab the brown menu and open it, my eyes scanning to see what they serve here.

I'm not sitting here for more than a minute when the waiter comes to the table, pouring water into the two glasses on the table. "My name is Henry, and I'll be your server for the evening. Can I start you off with a cocktail while you wait?"

"Oh, that sounds so good. I'll have two." I laugh, not really joking. "Give me two martinis, two olives with one ice cube."

"Very well," he says and nods at me. I giggle to myself, scanning the restaurant and people watching. I see a couple of men sitting at the bar facing me as they talk to each other. I look out at the street and watch as cars zoom through and around other cars. Henry comes over a couple of minutes later with two martinis on his tray. He places them both in front of me. I smile at him, raising a glass to him, then take a long gulp. Yup, no sipping here, not after the news I just got. "This is fantastic," I say. "I'll take another." He just nods and walks away, no doubt judging me in his head. But it's not every day you find out that your gay ex-boyfriend is engaged to another woman. I don't even think there is a greeting card for that shit, but I could be wrong.

I finish off the first martini in record time. The heat of the alcohol slowly creeps up, making my cheeks flustered. *I'm glad I took an Uber,* I think as I grab the second martini and bring it to my lips. I'm one sip into drinking my second martini when I see a man walk in the door, and the glass stops midair. The only thing going through my mind is *holy shit.*

His black suit molds to his body with a crisp white button-down shirt underneath, and he left the top two buttons open, showing a hint of his tan skin. His black aviator glasses hide his eyes, but it doesn't matter. His hair is cut short, his face is clean shaven, and his lips— oh my god, his lips are so full, which conjures an image of me sucking his bottom lip to run through my mind. I shake my head; it must be the vodka. "No more drinks for me," I say under my breath, looking down at the drink in my hand. Then I make the mistake of looking up again, and I see the woman at the hostess stand turn and look around the room.

Her eyes stop on me as she points at me, smiling at the man who doesn't even pay attention to her. He dips his head to her and makes his way over to me. I still can't see his eyes, but there is no denying that I feel his stare right through me. "Oh, shit," I whisper to myself, and as he comes closer, I see that his jaw is square, and his chest is wider than I thought. I don't think I inhale or exhale a breath while he walks around the tables, finally stopping at mine. He takes off his glasses, and I finally see his smoky gray eyes. "Are you Laney?"

I don't know what happens, but my throat closes. I try to talk, but no words come out of my mouth, so I don't say anything. My mouth opens and then closes again, but not a sound is made. Instead, the waiter comes back, smiling. "Here are two more." I look at who I think is my blind date as he glares at the man, and I laugh nervously.

"It isn't what it looks like," I tell the man standing beside the table.

"Really? I find it hard to believe. It looks like you're sitting here waiting for something bad to happen." He then looks around, eyeing everyone in the place, and it's a good thing I'm not standing because my legs would give out.

Chapter Four

Hunter

I get into my Range Rover and grab my glasses, sliding them on as I wait for the air conditioning to start. Pulling out, I make my way over to the Ivy Garden. As soon as Anthony left, I got on Google and searched to see how long one should stay on a blind date. The answer was straightforward—it should be for a drink or coffee—so I'm thinking thirty minutes if I order something that is served right away like water. Not one to take any chances, I have my phone set to ring thirty minutes after I arrive for good measure.

I pull up to the front door, and the valet meets me at my door once I stop. "Good evening, sir," he says once I open my door.

"Yeah, I won't be here long," I tell him as I get out, not bothering to take off my sunglasses when I hand him the keys.

"No worries, sir. It will be here when you are ready," he says, handing me the ticket for later. I put it in the inside pocket of my suit jacket. I walk inside to the hostess table, where a woman who looks like she is eighteen stands smiling.

"How may I help you?" she asks sweetly. I stop and look around to see if I might recognize the woman I'm here to meet, even though I've never met her. I spot a couple of women at the bar, but I instinctively know they aren't her. I also check for exits. It's not my fault; it's just instilled in me.

Looking to the left, I don't see anyone sitting alone, but then I look to the right, and I see her. I don't know why I know it's her, but I just do. With curly long blond hair, she downs a martini, then picks up another one and brings it to her mouth. I spot a waiter walking with two more martinis on his tray, and I'm not surprised when I see him approaching her table. "Great," I say under my breath. "I found her," I tell the hostess and start walking toward the table. She spots me and watches my every move. Luckily, the glasses I'm wearing stop her from seeing my eyes.

The closer I get to her, the more my pulse speeds up. What the fuck? This is weird. I look around maybe to see if something else is piquing my interest or maybe I spotted something to elevate my pulse, but no, it's her. The fact that a gorgeous woman is sitting by herself and drinking like a fish is enough to get any man's adrenaline pumping. Isn't it?

"Are you Laney?" I ask, taking off my glasses, and

my gray eyes finally meet her blue ones. She opens her mouth, expecting, I think, something to come out, but nothing does. I continue looking around to see if anyone is watching her, and it's no surprise that I spot two guys at the bar sizing her up.

"Here are two more." The waiter smiles at her, putting two more glasses down on the table and taking the two now empty ones away. She laughs nervously, and I want to reach out and trip him when he walks away.

"It isn't what it looks like." Her soft voice breaks me out of my plan, and I turn back to her as she smiles at me, causing my heartbeat to skyrocket. The collar of my shirt suddenly feels tight, but it's not even buttoned.

"Really? I find it hard to believe," I finally say. Looking around again, I spot the same two guys in suits sitting at the bar watching her. This time, one of them spots me and looks back down at his drink. "It looks like you're sitting here waiting for something bad to happen." I pull out the chair and sit in front of her.

"Um." She still doesn't say anything.

"How is it a good idea for a single, gorgeous woman to be sitting by herself, drowning in martinis?" I ask her, and she finally talks.

"I don't usually drink." I am not sure if I believe her or not, and me not saying anything gets her a little bit sassy. She crosses her arms over her chest. "What? A girl can't have a bad day?" she says, her voice getting louder. "Has that never, ever happened?"

Now it's my time to stutter. "Um. Do you know that drinking two or more drinks for a woman your size ..."

28

I look her up and down, and it's my downfall at that moment. "Your reflexes are cut in half, maybe even more," I say, finally making eye contact with the guy at the bar again. I don't have to say anything because he turns to his friend and starts talking to him.

"You think that just because I'm sitting here by myself waiting for a blind date …" she says and then takes another sip of her martini. "You think that just because I'm not with anyone, I can't drink?" I don't answer her. She clearly needs to discuss whatever is on her mind. "You think because my mother set me up on this date that I can't take care of myself? That I, an independent woman who owns her own business, can't sit at a table and have a drink or two, or three?"

I raise my hand and call the waiter over. He rushes over with a smile that goes away fast when my tone comes out less than friendly. "Bring us water and some bread," I tell him, "and no more martinis."

"Um," Laney says, leaning over and turning to the waiter, "he's not the boss of me. If I want another martini, you bring me another one." Her cheeks are pink, and I'm wondering if it's because she's mad or if it's from the alcohol. Either way, I like it.

"We'll just take the check," I tell him, and I reach into my jacket pocket. Grabbing my wallet, I open it and pull out the black AmEx card. I look over at her. "Do you come here often?"

"What is happening right now?" she says, turning to look around.

I look outside at my car, then turn to look at her.

29

"This is what is going to happen." I lean forward to get closer to her. "I'm going to pay the bill. We are going to get up and leave, and I'm going to drive you home."

She leans back in her chair, crossing her arms over her chest and rolling her eyes. "This is insane," she says, but I don't bother answering her because the waiter approaches with the bill.

"Sixty-seven dollars for four martinis," I mutter under my breath as I sign my name, then get up and reach my hand out for her. She looks at my hand, debating whether to take it. "It's a helping hand. You don't want to take it, then don't, but we're still leaving." I put my hands in my pockets. "Choice is yours."

She grabs the napkin that was on her lap and throws it on the table, then stands up suddenly. The martinis must hit her because she wobbles a bit and grabs the table to steady herself. I raise my hand to grab her, but when she turns her head and leers at me, I step back, motioning with my hand for her to walk ahead of me. She walks with her head held high, putting one foot in front of the other, and I watch her ass sway. I nod to the hostess who smiles at us, and luckily, I see my car hasn't been moved. The valet smiles at me, grabbing my keys. "You weren't lying about being long," he says. Laney looks at me and mouths, "Wow."

I grab the keys and walk to the passenger side of the car to open the door for Laney. "You know I can simply put you over my shoulder and shove you in." She walks to the car and gets in. The whole time, she looks like she is killing me in her head, and chances are, she probably is.

I slam the door closed and walk over to the driver's side and get in. I turn on the car and then finally turn back and look at her. I'm about to say something, but her scent has now filled the car, and I'm not sure what I would say. The smell of citrus hits me, and I look over at her. "Where do you live?" I ask her and wait as she turns to look at me. Folding her arms over her chest, she leans her back against the door.

"You think I'm going to give a stranger my home address?" She pffts. "No way. But nice try there."

I laugh and then turn to look at her, copying her stance with a smirk. "You won't give me, a perfect stranger, your address, but you will get into my car?" I shake my head.

"Oh my god!" she yells. "This is not happening to me. Not today," she says, trying to open the door, but I put the car in drive. She just looks at me as I smile and drive away from the curb. "You just kidnapped me," she says.

"See what drinking can do? You aren't on alert, not on the ball," I tell her as I make my way to the beach where they have a small restaurant that I love. "You got into a car with a complete stranger. Now, I can take you wherever I want."

"You're not a complete stranger," she says, and I look over at her. "Our mothers know each other. So, if anything happens to me, she knows where to look."

"Yes, but your mother doesn't know me," I tell her. "Do you know any serial killers who actually told their mothers they were serial killers?" I ask her and wait for her to answer me. "Do you think Jeffrey Dahmer went home and said, 'Hey, Mom, I just ate a human today, can I have some rice with my chicken?'"

"Well, there may be. Who knows, maybe he did, and she thought he was joking," she says, and I just shake my head.

Once we get to the parking lot, I park and look out the window at the water. From our parking spot, you can't see where the path leads you.

"Here's what's going to happen. We are going to get out, I'm going to get you something to eat and sober you up as much as I can, then I'll drive you home."

She grunts and opens the door. "I'll be sure to tell my mother how nice you are," she says and slams the door. She walks around the car, and I get out, meeting her at the back of the car.

"This way," I say as I lead her by her elbow to the secluded little restaurant. We walk down the pebbled sanded pathway, the trees shading the sunset, and approach the entrance of the secluded little restaurant. Unless you know it's here, you would never stop.

"What is this place?" Laney asks. She looks around, her eyes going right and left as she takes in everything. I know the restaurant looks more like a shack with its yellow aluminum siding and chipped paint. The blue roof looks like it will fly away with a gust of wind, and the two white plastic tables outside have seen better days.

"This is where I bring my victims," I say, smiling at

her. She pushes me away, mumbling, "Asshole," under her breath as she walks forward. I get to the door before her, so I reach out and pull it open, the creaking louder than the waves. The smell of spices hits us right away when we walk in.

I follow Laney's eyes as she looks around the restaurant. An aqua colored L-shaped bar sits in the middle of the room with six wooden barstools. The colors of the Mexican flag decorate the back of the bar, and glass shelves hold up bottles of tequila and rum.

On the side of the bar sits four tables like the ones outside but with red and green tablecloths. But she isn't looking at that; she is looking at the wall of windows across the back that lead out to the covered terrace only steps away from the beach. "Let's sit outside," I suggest, and she just nods at me, walking toward the glass doors.

When we walk farther into the restaurant, Guadalupe comes out from the kitchen and meets us. "Oh, look who comes back to see me." She smiles at me, and I walk over, bending to kiss the fifty-year-old four-foot-ten lady who owns this restaurant. "This is a nice surprise," she says, looking past me and straight at Laney.

"We are going to sit outside," I tell her, and she just smiles at me and nods her head, walking back into the kitchen. When I walk to the back door and slide it open, the first thing you hear is the waves crashing on the beach. I wait for Laney to step out and look around. The beauty just stops you in your tracks. The outside porch area is shaded by trees, and the lanterns hanging in the branches emit a soft glow. The same lanterns line a path leading down to the beach.

"This is so beautiful," she says softly, and I turn to look at her. Her pink cheeks are gone, replaced by a softness in her face. She kicks off her wedges and walks off the wooden terrace to the beach. I don't follow her. Instead, I watch as she walks down the sand to the shore and waits for the water to rush up over her feet. She just stands there, the wind blowing her hair to the side and her dress flying with it.

"I brought you something to drink," Guadalupe says. "But no alcohol for you," she says to me when she puts down two glass pitchers of margaritas. "This one has the tequila in it," she says, pointing at the other pitcher with the lemons around it.

"Can you take that one back?" I tell her, and then I hear Laney right beside me.

"Oh, no, you don't," she says, walking past me to her chair. Her feet covered in wet sand, she pulls out one of the wooden chairs and sits down, facing the ocean. She looks up at Guadalupe. "Can I have extra salt in mine?"

"Of course, my dear." She smiles at Laney, and then looks at me. "If she isn't safe with you, then who is she safe with?" The question rocks me as I stare at Laney, who looks at me as if she just won the war.

Chapter Five

Laney

I watch him, almost as if I'm taunting him to tell me no, but he doesn't. The vein in his head looks like it's going to explode, his jaw so tight it looks like he's going to snap, but he just nods at Guadalupe, and she walks away, trying to hide her smile.

I roll my eyes at him as he comes over and finally shrugs his suit jacket off. Shit, maybe this isn't a good idea. My mouth gets dry when his fingers unsnap the button at his wrist. My heart beats a bit faster when he rolls up his sleeves, and I see his watch and tanned and smooth arms. He sits in the chair in front of me, and my eyes are still on his arms and the way his muscles pop when he bends his elbows. His body faces both the door and the beach as he takes in the place all around us.

"Just because it's only the two of us, don't think you're going to get shitfaced," he says, and right then, whatever spell I was under that he was hot is off the table. Okay, fine, he's still hot, but he's an asshole.

"I can see it," I tell him, picking up the pitcher and pouring myself a margarita. Taking a long gulp, I'm sure he glares at me, but his sunglasses once again shield his eyes. "Mmm, that's good," I say, putting it down and then looking back at him. "As I was saying, I see it."

He puts one foot on his knee and leans back, resting his hands on his stomach, his fingers entwined. A stomach I'm quite sure doesn't contain one ounce of fat. "What can you see?" he asks while he just looks at me.

"Why your mother has to set you up on dates," I tell him and take another sip until nothing is left. Guadalupe appears as I'm pouring another margarita, placing two small bowls on the table. I see one is with salsa and the other one with queso. Then she places a bigger bowl in the middle with tortilla chips.

"Here, this is to start," she says, grabbing the pitcher and pouring me another one. She winks at me, and I smile at her. I grab a tortilla chip, and it's still warm. "I just made those."

I dip the chip in the queso, scooping some of the cheese, and pop it in my mouth. The flavors sink into my tongue, the warm cheese sauce with the spices making me close my eyes and moan. "This is the best thing I've ever tasted in my life."

"I like her," she says, looking over at Anthony, and she walks away.

"See, at least someone likes me today," I tell him. I grab another chip—not even caring if it's not ladylike at this point—dip it and toss it in my mouth. It's very clear that we will not be going on date number two. That is for sure.

"So, you think I can't get dates?" he asks, and it annoys me that his glasses are still on, and I can't see his eyes.

"What's up with the *Men in Black* attire?" I ask him. "It's not even sunny, so you can lose the glasses."

"*Men in Black*?" I don't know if he's asking me a question or not, so I just shrug.

"I really hope you have the pen thingamajig and can erase this evening from my mind," I tell him, and he puts his head back and laughs, the sound making me smile.

"I get it now," he finally says. When he takes off his glasses, I have to say I wish he hadn't. His gaze hits me right in the stomach, and the butterflies start. I shake my head because I don't think it's possible; it's probably the tequila. I mean, it has to be, right? I look down and then look up at him again, and there it is again, the gaze of his gray eyes. "So why do you think my mother needs to set me up on dates?" he asks. He sits up, grabbing a chip and dipping it in the salsa.

"Well," I start. At first, I try to choose my words carefully, but then I realize who cares what I say. "Besides the fact you aren't all that friendly, you are definitely rude and condescending." He smirks at me, and I continue, "And irritating. So flipping irritating."

"Is that all?" he asks me, almost like he's baiting me. Waiting for me to lose my shit. Instead, I shake my head. Something about the way he looks at me makes me lower my guard.

"I had a shitty day," I tell him even though I know I shouldn't. "I found out my ex is engaged today."

"Why do you care?" he asks, and I try not to throw something at him. I actually look around for something, but the only thing I think I could throw is the margarita, and well, I'm not wasting that on him. "Why should you care? He's your ex for a reason," he prods.

"I don't care," I say louder than I expected to and slam my hand on the table. "I could give two rats' asses if he's getting married."

"So then why is it shitty?" he asks, taking another chip and dipping it in the salsa.

"Because he's gay!" I yell; his eyes go big, and his mouth drops opens and then closes. "Yeah, what?" I cock my head to the side. "No comeback?" He doesn't say anything. He just waits for me to finish my rant. "I walked in on him nailing his assistant, who was a man, in case you didn't put two and two together."

"He's gay?" he finally says, shocked.

"Who knows?" I say. "Maybe he's bi." I take another long gulp of my margarita. "Maybe my vagina pushed him over the edge."

"I don't think your vagina had anything to do with it," he says, looking toward the door as Guadalupe walks out with two more bowls.

"Homemade guacamole, chunky and smooth," she says, putting it down on the table and topping off my margarita again. I take a chip and dip it into the guacamole. Popping it into my mouth, I moan. The smoothness of the avocado with the tart of the lemon and flavor of the cilantro make this guacamole hands down the best I've ever eaten.

"I lied," I tell her. "This is the best thing I've ever had in my whole life." She laughs at me and pats my hand, then walks away. "How isn't there not a line to get into this restaurant?" I look around at the emptiness of the restaurant.

"She isn't listed in the Yellow Pages," he tells me and takes a sip of his virgin margarita. "So, your gay ex-boyfriend is getting married?"

"Yes," I tell him, eating another chip. "And to a woman, no less."

"Does she know?" He asks me the same question I've asked myself a thousand times since I found out.

"I have no idea." I shrug my shoulders. "I don't speak to any of his family. His sister kept in touch with me when we first broke up, but then it was awkward, so I stopped really talking to her."

"Are you going to tell her?" he asks.

"No way." I shake my head. "Not a chance in hell."

"So, what if it was you?" he asks me, and I look at him. "What if you were marrying this man, thinking that he was your forever, but instead, he's living a lie and now so are you," he points out. "Would you not want someone to tell you?"

"Yes," I say, leaning back in my chair, "but I don't think it's my place."

He chuckles. "I think the ex-girlfriend walking in on

him drilling his boyfriend is the perfect person. At least in my opinion."

"He really was drilling him." I laugh at the way he said it. I look at him as he takes another chip. The sun setting makes the hanging lights brighten a bit more. His gray eyes almost look darker. "So why are you still single?" I sit up, fold my arms on the table, and watch him.

"Not five minutes ago, you just told me why I was still single. I believe you said I was not friendly." He laughs, leaning back into the chair.

"Yup," I agree, drinking another sip of my never-ending margarita, thanks to Guadalupe topping it off every time she returns. "Although I don't think I used the word unfriendly." I smile at him. "We could add it to the list."

"Rude," he says. His voice is getting softer, or I might be getting drunk.

"Yes, and don't forget condescending"—I point at him—"and irritating." I laugh. "Irritating should be listed twice."

"How can I forget those?" He smiles softly at first and then fully, his eyes lighting up in the dimness of the patio. He doesn't say anything more nor do I because Guadalupe comes out with platters of food.

"It smells so good," I say as she sets down the plates on another table next to us. Anthony gets up and moves the chairs away from the table, picking it up and placing it next to the one we are sitting at.

Guadalupe smiles at him and pats his back when he

goes back to sit down. "I made three different tacos," she says, pointing at the three plates with five soft tacos on each. "Pork," she says, pointing at the meat that looks like it's been shredded with a fork, little cubes of onion and some lime wedges beside them. "Beef," she says, pointing at the ground meat with shredded cheddar cheese, some salsa, and a little sour cream. "And fish." Golden pieces of white fish with pico de gallo and what looks like little pieces of mango. My mouth waters as I look at the food. "Tamales …" And I stop listening to her, my fingers itching to grab one of those fish tacos.

"Can I eat yet?" I ask her, and she just laughs, nodding.

I grab one of the fish tacos and eat it, the flavors of lime and cumin hitting my lips. "I'm coming back here tomorrow," I say, chewing. "Honest to god"—I drink another sip—"this is the best meal I've had in all my life."

He looks over at me, chewing on his own bite of taco. "You're welcome." He smirks as he chews, and we don't say anything while we eat. I just savor it because what started as a shitty day ended not so shitty. I wouldn't tell him that, but it wasn't so bad.

I lean back in my chair. "I'm so happy I didn't wear pants tonight," I say, laughing while I take another sip of my margarita. Noticing that my pitcher is empty, I look over at him. "I think I'm drunk." He looks up, raising one eyebrow. "Off food, you jerk." I laugh at his expression. "It's safe to say you aren't going to attack me and eat my insides."

"How do you know?" he says. "Maybe this is me setting the scene?"

"Oh, please." I roll my eyes. "You crossed me off the list the minute you walked in and saw two martinis in front of me." I look at the door as it opens and watch as Guadalupe comes out with a fresh pitcher in her hand. I throw up my hand in victory as he throws his head back and moans. She grabs the empty pitcher, nodding and smiling at us as she walks back inside.

"I didn't cross anything off," he says, waiting for the door to close. I sit up this time, grabbing the pitcher and pouring another drink. This time, I'm drinking it slower.

It could be the tequila talking, or it could be the fact that I just don't care tonight, but I say, "I could be sitting here full on naked, and you still wouldn't touch me." His eyes narrow to slits. "Let me enjoy myself, will you? This is the 'my gay ex is getting married and my blind date was a bust' celebration." I get up, grabbing the new pitcher that Guadalupe placed on the table, and walk out to the beach. My feet hit the cold sand, and I focus on walking to the shore without falling. I place the pitcher in the sand and then hold my skirt down while I sit on the cold sand. I don't even have to look back to know he followed me. "You can be a Neanderthal, but at least your chivalry isn't dead," I say, bringing my knees to my chest as I watch the now dark blue ocean go through its own fight as the waves roll onto the sand with a crashing sound.

"What kind of date would I be if I let my date drown?" he says, sitting next to me. I look over at him and laugh. He's sitting on the beach with a suit, socks, and dress shoes.

"You didn't even take your shoes off." I throw my head back as my feet slip, and I hold my stomach while I laugh, and he rolls his eyes. "This turned out to be an okay date, Anthony," I say, watching him, and he looks at me.

"Call me T," he tells me curtly, then he turns and looks at the ocean, and I watch him.

"Oh, is that a nickname?" I ask him, and he just nods, still not looking at me.

"Yeah," he says one word, one syllable.

"You're okay, T," I tell him and then turn back to look at the water. We sit here for what feels like forever when I finally get up and grab the pitcher and the glass. "I guess I brought this down here for nothing," I say, looking at the still full pitcher.

He gets up, dusting off his pants, and then grabs the pitcher from me, and I follow him back up. I notice that the inside lights are off. "Where is Guadalupe?" I turn and ask him.

"She locks up at eight." He puts the pitcher in a sink I never even noticed in the corner, then turns on the water and rinses it out. He grabs a towel hanging beside the sink to dry his hands.

"I didn't even get to pay her," I tell him, grabbing my wedges and sitting to dust the sand off my shoes.

"I paid her," he says, and I'm not the least bit surprised. He can be rude, but he's respectful. Once I have my shoes on, I stand and go to him. "Are you cold?" he asks me when a gust of wind comes through, and I shiver. I just nod.

He takes his jacket and wraps it around my shoulders. I reach out my hand to hold the jacket closed as he holds my arm and we walk down the path back to his car.

He leads me to the passenger side and opens the door for me, and as I get in, not a word is uttered. I watch him walk around to his side, my stomach doing a sudden flip. He opens the door. "So where do you live?" he asks, looking at me.

I lean my head back on the seat. "I'm not supposed to give my address out to strangers." I laugh when he smirks. "Someone I know would be really, really mad if I did give you my address."

"You should listen to that guy. He sounds really, really smart," he says, turning on the car while I laugh and give him my address. I turn my head to the side, watching the scenery outside while he makes his way to my condo. I watch people walking on the street, and I watch the waves hitting the shore, the ocean looks black. The blinking of lights from a ship in the distance is all I can see.

He pulls up in front of my condo complex, and I unsnap my seat belt. My hand reaches for the door handle while I turn and look at him. "This night has turned out surprisingly better than I expected it to," I tell him as I peel his jacket away from my shoulders. "Thank you, T."

I pull on the handle, opening the door and taking one last look at him. "It really was fun," I say, getting out and walking away from him. I turn to wave at him, and I'm not surprised to find him standing in front of his car, leaning back on the hood. "You're also annoying," I tell him over my shoulder, and he smiles with his arms crossed over his chest. I walk into my condo and close the door, listening for his car door to close, then for him to drive away. I don't turn on any lights. I just lock the front door and double check that the back door is locked. Making my way into my bedroom, I go straight to my bathroom, swinging my feet into the tub and taking off my shoes. The grains of sand falling with little clinks in the tub. I turn the water on, checking the temperature with my hand, then put my feet under the water when it's just the right temperature. The whole time, my mind replays the date or non-date in my head.

I dry my feet and slip out of my dress, pulling off the cover and sliding into bed. I fix my pillows all around me, sinking into one, and as my mind drifts back again and again, I fall asleep to the picture of him leaning over in the car and kissing me.

Chapter Six

Hunter

I let myself into my house, and the quietness greets me as I toss my keys on the table beside the door. I kick off my shoes and walk directly upstairs.

The cold shower is exactly what I need. Putting my hands on the marble shower, I duck my head so the water can run over the muscles in my neck. One date with that woman had me strung up so tight I thought my neck would snap.

The way she pushed me at every corner, it took everything I had not to take her over my shoulder and tie her up until she caved. Meanwhile, I would worship her body. "Fuck," I say when my cock, which finally went down after two hours, is up again and straining. I wrap my hand around myself, the water getting colder and colder, but I don't stop until I spill with her face on my mind.

Once I get into my bed, it takes me two seconds to fall asleep, but then sleep comes to me for just a couple of hours. For the rest of the night, I'm tossing and turning. When five o'clock hits and I've already been awake for an hour, I give up. I pull on my shorts and go downstairs. Sitting outside, I watch the sun come up while I work.

By seven o'clock, I get up and slide on a T-shirt, my socks, and my running shoes. Getting in the car, I drive to the beach where I like to run. After parking my truck, I get out and hold each foot up to stretch. Then I take off, pushing myself the whole way but especially the last mile just for fun. Usually when I run, all my thoughts are buried. I clear my mind, and it's nothing but the push to run. This time, by the beach, each time my foot hit the hard, wet sand, I heard her laughter ring in my head. I heard her sass, her fucking sass, and I heard the softness in her voice when I wasn't pissing her off. No matter how many times I try to clear my head, my mind keeps replaying the night before with Laney and her sass. I haven't had that much fun with a woman … well, since ever.

I finally make my way back to my car, my chest heaving when I stop and sit on the sand because the rising sun is starting to heat fast. I look around as families start making their way to the beach. The mother carrying the kids while the father lugs the chairs and the umbrellas, no doubt cursing in his head.

I stop at the little shack on the beach and grab two ice-cold water bottles, draining one before I get in the car and another one as soon as I sit in the car and open the windows to let the heat out. My chest still heaves as I work my heartbeat to get back to normal. I'm about to press the start button when I hear a buzz coming from somewhere in the car. I take my phone out of my pocket and look at it, but it's no surprise that no one has called or sent a text. I put my phone in the cup holder and start the car, rolling down the windows and letting some of the heat out.

I wait a couple of minutes for the air conditioning to cool the car down some, then close the window. I pull out of the parking lot, but then I hear the buzz again. I look around, not sure what the hell is going on, but then I hear a beep and realize

it's coming from between the seats.

I slide my hand between the seats and pull out a huge white iPhone with a marble looking case on it and a sparkly button on the back. I don't even have to wonder whose it is. I look down and see that it already has ten missed calls and a text message. *What in the hell?* I scroll down to check the notification, and when I press the middle button, the phone automatically opens with a picture of the beach in the background. I click on the green message box with a red number of twenty in the corner. I see a bunch of messages—a couple from her mother, one from a Sandy, but the one that is on the top is under the name Me.

If you are reading this, can you please return my phone to the following address. REWARD WILL BE GIVEN!

"What is wrong with her?" I ask myself aloud, shaking my head. She actually just gave her address away.

I make my way home to shower, pulling on a pair of blue jeans and grabbing a simple white T-shirt. Sliding on my white Adidas running shoes, I grab my sunglasses and the phone in question. I look down at it and see she has sent another text. This time all in caps as though she's yelling at this person who found her phone.

EVEN IF YOU DON'T RETURN IT, CAN YOU AT LEAST ANSWER ME THAT YOU HAVE IT?

This woman is out of her mind, I think as I lock up my house. I get into my car and make my way over to her house. I park exactly where I did last night, getting out and locking the car over my shoulder. Jogging up the stairs to her apartment, I knock once. I wait for her to ask who is there, but she doesn't. Instead, she opens the door, and my mouth gapes open.

She's standing there, her long blond hair hanging over one shoulder, her blue eyes crystal clear. Not a trace of makeup; she needs nothing. My eyes roam up and down her body as she stands there in silky pale pink shorts and a tank with white lace. The matching pale pink robe hangs open, covering nothing. "What the hell are you wearing?" I ask her, and she looks at me and then down at my hand and squeals, jumping up and down. "Can you not do that?" I ask her between clenched teeth.

"You found my phone," she says, reaching for it, and I see that it's the same color as her outfit. "Thank you so much. Where did you find it?" I'm about to answer her when she says, "Oh, wait, come in. I was just making breakfast." She doesn't even wait for me to answer before she just walks away from the door, leaving it wide open. I watch her walk down the white hallway, putting the phone on her counter and then grabbing her hair and tying it on the top of her head. I have an internal debate with myself about going in or not, but my feet move before my head can catch up on the argument.

"Someone needs to discuss the dangers of today with her," I say under my breath. I follow the same path she did and see the white plush couch against the wall with two gray plush chairs on each side. I look for the television but don't see one.

I continue and see that she is in her kitchen at the stove doing who knows what. "What are you doing?" I look at her kitchen, and it's no surprise it's also white. The only color is the beige counters. The kitchen is a small square once you walk in to it. The counter goes all around, only stopping at the stainless-steel stove on the left and then the sink sits right under the little window, that has a small pot of flowers on the sill. The counter continues till you get to the stainless-steel fridge.

From my side of the counter, I see she has two frying pans out. "I'm making huevos rancheros," she tells me. Turning to open one of the cabinets, she takes out two square white plates. "It's a good thing you showed up because I made way too much." She puts the plates on the counter, then grabs one of the frying pans and starts to distribute the food. She loads my plate with more food than hers, grabbing the second frying pan and placing what looks like turkey bacon on her plate. Then she opens the oven and grabs a mitt, reaching in and taking out a small tray with bacon and sausage. She places three slices of bacon on my plate and then puts two sausage links on hers.

"Laney," I say, putting my hands on my hips. My mouth waters, and my stomach rumbles. "We need to discuss a couple of things." I'm trying to keep calm, but when she looks at me and smiles, my mind goes blank. The whole part of me determined to give her a firm lecture is almost gone.

"Do you want a mimosa?" she asks me as she grabs the plates. "Can you grab the OJ and champagne?" She shrugs her shoulders, tossing her head to the side at the fridge. "Meet you outside on the patio."

I watch her walk out onto the patio, placing the plates down on the table, and then she turns and comes back in. "I'll get the utensils." She walks past me, her silky robe flying back a bit as she walks, and it hits my hand, my fingers moving when she moves away. "Do you want hot sauce?" she asks when she gets back into the kitchen, opening the drawer to grab forks and knives. Then she leans up, her top rising a bit to reveal a little skin, and I'm at a loss for words. "Don't forget our drinks," she says, walking past me, still fucking smiling. I just look up and think that this is God's way of getting back at me for something. Maybe because I never called my mother back. But whatever it is, please forgive me.

"There has to be a reason," I whisper, walking into the kitchen. Opening her fridge, I grab the orange juice and champagne. "Do you need glasses?" I shout, hoping she hears me, and when I don't get an answer, I open the cabinets till I find the glasses and carry two outside.

I have no idea what I'm going to find, but I'm not expecting her patio to be so cozy. She has a small L-shaped patio set with huge plush pillows. A small table in the front of it has two candles. I look over at Laney, and she is sitting at her small square table with two chairs, looking out at the ocean. "It's such a pretty day," she says, looking at me. "It's going to be a hot one, I think."

I sit in front of her, scanning the place with my eyes and watching the door again. "Laney," I say, then watch as she picks up the champagne and pours herself some and then tops it off with orange juice. "I don't even know where to start with you," I say honestly.

She laughs at me, throwing her head back. Her bare neck open for me to lean in and bite, then slowly suck. "Well"—she picks up her glass and holds it up—"considering this is our second date, you should start with last night was awesome." She brings the glass to her mouth and takes a sip.

I look at her, and I feel my blood pressure rise. I put my hands in front of me flat on the table. "You gave a total stranger your address." I shake my head.

She looks at me confused. "How did I do that?"

"You sent your address to your phone," I tell her. "Why?"

"Well, for one, my phone is locked, so no one can steal my information," she says, taking a sip of her drink.

"It isn't locked. I got into it just by pressing the button. Nice screensaver," I tell her and expect her to be shocked or maybe surprised, but she isn't either of those things.

Instead, she shrugs her shoulders and puts her drink down. "Well, I didn't know where I left it, so I thought maybe if I sent myself a message, the person who found it could bring it back to me," she says, opening her hands in front of her in an "obviously, I had a plan" gesture.

"What if I was a serial murderer?" I ask her again. "Or I was trafficking women?"

"Oh my god." She rolls her eyes. "Seriously, I knew I either left it in your car or at Guadalupe's."

"How could you have been so sure?" I ask her, and she laughs at me again.

"Because I sent my best friend a text when I got in your car," she tells me, and I don't know what to say. "You know, after you came into the restaurant and went all apeshit on me about drinking?"

"I didn't go apeshit on anyone. I merely ..." She holds her hand up, stopping me.

"You went apeshit," she says and then continues. "Anyway, I sent her my location when we got to the restaurant. You know, in case you were an actual serial killer," she says, laughing.

I pick up my fork and point it at her. "You're a nutcase, you know that, right?" She just shrugs.

"I may be, but what does it say about you, coming back for a second date?" she points out as she grabs a forkful of eggs, eating it and then saying, "I have to say

I like this look better than the suit." She moves her wrist up and down, pointing at me with her fork.

"Good to know," I say, grabbing a forkful of my own egg and eating it before I tell her that I like her outfit way better than yesterday, too. I'm trying to be a gentleman and not notice that her nipples are pebbled and waiting to be pinched. I shake my head.

"So, what do you want to do today?" she asks me, then continues to talk. "There is a food truck festival I've never been to. Do you want to do that?"

Everything is telling me to say no and walk away. She doesn't even know my real name because she thinks I'm Anthony. I came to return her phone and tell her how stupid it was to share her information with a stranger. She could tell her mother that she had a semi nice date, and that I was a gentleman. "Sure," my mouth says before my brain catches up to it.

"Great. I'll go change, and we can head out." She smiles at me, and once I see her smile, I don't have the heart to tell her that I can't go.

She gets up and grabs her plate, putting her utensils in the middle and bringing it inside. She comes back out. "I got it," I tell her, and she just nods at me.

"I'll go get dressed and be right back out," she says, turning and walking back inside.

I gather the plates and bring them into the kitchen, rinsing them and putting them in the dishwasher as I battle the thoughts inside my head. On one hand, I'm thinking, *why can't I go? I'm not Anthony*. While on the other hand, I'm thinking how great this will look when

Anthony's mother gets the phone call that we went out on back-to-back dates.

"I'm ready." I hear her say, walking into the room. I look at her, and nothing, I mean nothing, will stop me from taking her out today. She's wearing white cut-off shorts, leaving her long tan legs on full display. Her shirt is a loose cold shoulder V-neck with spaghetti straps but also long sleeves. Her hair hangs down to her waist in long curls. Strappy gold sandals complete the look. "Is this okay?" she says, and I just nod.

"Yeah, it's fine," I tell her. "You might get hot," I say, looking at her long sleeves.

"It's okay. I'm wearing a bikini top under this shirt." She grabs her oversized bag. "Shall we?" she says, sliding on her big sunglasses. She looks like a model stepping outside the magazine.

I let her lead the way out, turning to watch her lock her door. "See? I'm safe," she says, putting her keys in her bag and coming to my side.

I laugh as we walk down the steps together and get in the car. I turn on the air conditioner. "It's really hot," she says, reaching behind her and grabbing her seat belt. "I've always wanted to go to this food truck thing," she says with a smile, "but no one ever wanted to go with me."

"I've never even heard about this," I tell her. "Where is this place?" I ask her. She grabs her phone to pull up the address, then I put it in my GPS and wait for it to calculate the route. I pull out of her parking lot and follow the directions. When I look over and see her looking out the window, I ask her the question I've been thinking about this whole time. "How did you text yourself this morning with no phone?"

"My iPad," she says, looking over at me. "I have iMessage set up on there also, so I texted myself."

"What if you had dropped it on the street by accident?" I ask her. "What if I wasn't the one who had it? Do you know what could have happened?"

She shrugs. "I was hoping it was you."

I turn and look at her. "What?" I ask her, shocked. "You hated me last night," I tell her, laughing.

"I didn't hate you at the end of the night. Your broodiness grew on me," she says, looking out the window again.

"Laney." I say her name softly, and she turns back, her lips forming a shy smile. "I don't think this is a good idea."

"Anthony," she starts saying, and I shake my head. *Fuck no.* There is no fucking way she is going to call me Anthony.

"If we do this thing today, you call me T," I tell her. I'd rather her call me asshole than someone else's name.

"Fine. T," she says, "how about this? I won't even tell my mother about this second date. We will leave it at we had coffee and decided to speak some other time."

I want to say no. My head is saying this isn't a good idea, but my car just leads us to this festival. I follow the herd of cars to the parking area. I park the car, and then just as fast as I park, another car parks next to me. I get out of the car, lock the door, and meet her at the back of the car. I look around, scoping out the exit routes. "You do that all the time." I hear her say as I look at the giant parking lot.

"Come on, let's go," she says as she takes my hand in hers and leads the way. When we walk through the gates, a woman hands us each a map of the festival. I look down and see that there are over a hundred food trucks. "I don't even know where to start," she says, and I look up at her.

"You always start at one end and go to the other." I look down at the map. We walk to the right of the map and look down the path, food trucks on each side of us. Each food truck has a canopy over their ordering window and three white plastic tables in front of them for people to sit down. We walk down the path, looking at the different foods. She doesn't release my hand, and I don't release hers as we walk from truck to truck.

"We should try at least one thing per row," she says, looking at the map with the hand that isn't holding mine. "Fried Oreo is my pick," she says, folding her map and placing it in her purse. "You choose your pick."

I look down and scan the first two rows. "If we are going with fried Oreos, I think we should try the mac and cheese." I look up at the menu for the food truck with the mac and cheese. "We are getting little portions, right?" I ask her, and she just nods her head.

"So, what do you think?" she asks while we stand here in line. "Traditional or lobster?" She looks up at me, and I look down at her, and the soft breeze blows her hair. With her hand in mine, I'm tempted to lean down and kiss her lips. I just stand here watching her, and she leans in a bit. I'm about to throw in the towel and lean forward when I hear the man.

"Next!" he yells, and I look at him. "What can I get you?"

"We'll have the small portion of the lobster mac and cheese," Laney answers and opens her purse to take out her money, and I look at her.

I release her hand and go into my wallet, pulling out a twenty. "Don't even think about that shit."

I don't need to see her eyes to know she is rolling them. "Simmer down there," she says, putting her hand on my chest.

The man hands me back my change with a number. "You're number seventy-five," he says, and I nod.

"Can we have two bottles of water please?" I ask him, giving him back the money. He reaches behind him and hands me two bottles of ice-cold water. "Go find a table," I tell her and watch as she walks to one of the three tables and grabs the one in the shade.

"Seventy-four and seventy-five!" the woman yells, and I step forward.

"I'm seventy-five," I say, and she hands me a small white cardboard container with two plastic forks sticking up from it. I smile at her and then turn to go to the table where Laney is sitting at.

I sit down next to her, and my eyes go to the entrance as I watch people come and go. "Okay, here we go," she says, grabbing one fork and then bringing it to her mouth. "Oh. My," she says, chewing and grabbing more, "this is hands down the best mac and cheese I've had in my life."

I grab my own fork and nod, eating a forkful. "Yup, it's pretty good," I say. I grab another forkful and stop eating.

I sit back in my chair and watch her take another bite. "That was so good," she says, and I look inside to see we ate half of it.

"There is half left," I tell her, and she leans back in her own chair, grabbing the water bottle and drinking it.

"Well, then have at it," she tells me, pointing at it. We stay at the table a couple of more minutes, and then I get up, grabbing the cardboard plate and taking it to the garbage. She joins me, then looks over at me. "Now on to that Oreo," she says, pointing at the truck and the little line forming in front of it. "I literally only want one," she says, though when we get to the front, she orders three.

"I thought you said you only wanted one?" I say after we step aside to wait for the order.

"I felt weird ordering just one when we are two people," she says, leaning, and I laugh at her. When our number is called, she steps up and grabs another white cardboard container and comes back. I look inside and see three golden deep-fried Oreos with white powdered sugar on them. "Okay, here goes," she says, grabbing one and biting half of it. I grab one myself, and my teeth bite through the puff pastry and sink into the softness of the cookie inside. The middle of the Oreo is melted and drips on my lips. "Ugh," I say. She laughs and leans forward to wipe my lip, and then she does the most erotic thing I've seen—well, today anyway. She takes the thumb she used on my lip and brings it to her mouth to suck it off. My cock springs into action before her thumb is even halfway to her lips.

"I think," she says once she takes her thumb out of her mouth, "that if you eat more than one of these, you can have a serious heart attack." I'm still looking at her lips. "Are you okay?" she asks, and I just nod. "Let's walk, so we can digest the seven thousand calories we just ate."

I nod my head again, and she reaches for my hand and pulls me along. We do the same things on the next row, sampling different things.

By the time we get to the third row, I think I'm going to throw up. "I can't eat anything else," I say, taking the last bite of the rib I was eating.

"You said that right before you ordered the ribs," she says, laughing at me as my bite of rib falls, and I move my foot out of the way so it falls on the ground instead of my shoe. I grab the napkin, then bend down and pick up the rib, walking to the trash where I toss it. I grab the wet wipe they gave us and wash off my hands. She walks next to me, putting one hand on my hip as she leans in to throw her own things out. Her little touches have been driving me crazy all day long, and if I thought I was tense yesterday, today is one for the records.

She's soft and funny and snarky, and she just makes me laugh. I put my hands on her hips, pulling her close to me. *Don't do anything stupid.* I hear my inner voice, yet I bend my head a touch. Her breath hitches, and I'm about to kiss her lips, but her phone buzzing in her pocket breaks the moment.

"Hello?" she says, answering the phone. "What?" She looks at me. "How bad?"

I look at her, now worried. "Can you drive me to my office?" she asks, and I nod right away, grabbing her hand and leading us to the car. "Okay, I'll be there in about twenty minutes."

"What's the matter?" I ask her when we get in the car, and she gives me the address to her office.

"My best friend, Sandy," she starts and then looks down and shakes her head. "She and her new boyfriend were trying out a sex swing." She looks at me. "It was one of those portable ones, and well, it snapped and …"

I put my hand to my mouth "Oh my god. Did he break his dick?" I ask, putting my other hand to my own crotch.

"No," she says, laughing. "He fell and knocked a tooth out. Before she got on it with him."

"You're a dentist?" I ask her and realize we never even spoke about what she does or what I do.

"Yeah," she says when I pull into a parking lot and see that little house of sorts. "This is my practice," she says with a smile on her face, reaching forward and opening the car door.

I get out with her, standing beside her when a car swings into the parking lot and parks beside us.

We stand here waiting, and I'm shocked when I see Anthony rounding the back of my car. I look at him, and he looks at me, and I look at Laney. "I can explain," I tell her right before all hell breaks loose.

"Hunter, what the hell are you doing here?" he says, holding an ice pack to his mouth.

"Hunter?" Laney looks over at me, her voice going soft. "Wait. What?"

"Laney, thank god you could meet us here," her friend, who I think is Sandy, says from beside Anthony. I look at the little girl with the pixie cut wearing shorts and a T-shirt. Anthony is wearing jeans and a white T-shirt and what looks like blood down the front. "Anthony, this is Laney." She introduces the two and Anthony looks at me and then at Laney, his eyes going wide.

"Holy shit, you're Laney?" Anthony says. "It was supposed to be one date." He looks at me, then back at Laney. "Jesus fuck. My mother is going to kill me," he says.

"What?" My eyes never leave Laney's as she looks from me to Anthony and then back again to me.

"I can explain." I go to her and put my hand on her arm as she shrugs me off.

"You lied to me," she says, and finally, Sandy shouts.

"What the fuck is going on right now?" She goes to Laney's side. "Who is this?" she asks her, and I swear I want to rewind the day and tell her the truth when I showed up at her front door.

"This is my blind date Anthony," Laney says, shaking her head, "or who I thought was my blind date, but he's just a liar." I've been to the war and I've been shot at more times than I care to admit, and I've broken bones, but these those four words just hurt me more.

Chapter Seven

Laney

I'm standing in the parking lot of my dental practice after one of the best dates I've ever been on, and it all comes crashing down that it was all a game and a lie. "He's just a liar," I say, and his eyes close and then open. I see the war going on in them, and I want to reach out.

"Let's go," I say to Anthony and then look at Sandy, turning around. Walking to the steps of my practice, I take my keys out of my purse, unlock the door, and turn off the alarm. "Take him to the second room, and I'll be right there," I say, heading to my office to grab my stuff.

"Laney, wait." I hear Anthony, or Hunter, as it's his real name, calling.

"I don't have time for this," I tell him, dumping my bag on my desk and grabbing my lab coat and my glasses with the magnifying glass. I turn and see him standing in the doorway. Why does he have to be so fucking dreamy when I'm supposed to hate him? "Move," I tell him, trying to walk past him, but he just stands there, blocking the way.

"Laney, let me explain." He tries again, and I just shake my head.

"No," I snap and then close my eyes. Tears threaten but I'm so angry right now that I keep them at bay. I open my eyes and look at him. "Explain what exactly?" I ask him. "How you duped me into pretending that you were someone else?" He just looks at me, and I don't give him a chance to speak. "How you pretended to give a shit about the date, knowing full well that you would never see me again? How you came in there pretending you were someone else, meanwhile probably laughing your ass over the poor girl who didn't know any better?"

"It isn't like that," he says, and I throw my hands up.

"It's exactly like that," I tell him. "You took me on a blind date that he didn't even have the balls to cancel. You sat at a table with me and had about fourteen meals, if we count all the food we ate today, and not once did you say, 'Laney, so there is this funny story that I want to tell you.' No, nothing like that."

"Laney!" I hear Sandy yell, and when he lets his guard down for a moment, I push past him, going to the room and seeing this man in the chair. "Will he break this chair?" she asks me, and I see his feet are way off. "I mean, he isn't really normal size."

"No, but we need X-rays before we even start," I tell her, and he nods, trying to get up. "Stay seated. I have X-ray machines in each room," I tell him, getting set up for the X-rays and waiting for it to be done. I grab the heavy blue vest, then walk over to him, and put it on him.

"So," he starts saying, "this is awkward." I glare at him.

"You didn't even have the decency to cancel the date or even show up and just brush me off," I snap at him, grabbing the white mouthpieces. I put on gloves and go back to him. "Bite down on this." He does, and I grab the machine to take his X-ray, placing the circle of the machine on the front of his mouth.

"Oh my god!" Sandy finally says out loud. "Is this the blind date you had yesterday?" She points at Hunter, who is still here, smiling. "High-five."

"No, no high-five," I say, putting her hand down when I walk past her. "He," I say, pointing at Anthony, who is sitting in the chair with his mouth pressed down on the bite block for the X-rays, "was supposed to be my blind date. He," I say, pointing at Hunter, who stands there with his arms crossed over his chest, "showed up and duped me by pretending to be him," I say, pointing back at Anthony, who looks at Sandy and shrugs his shoulders. "Everyone out of the room while I take the X-rays," I say, and they step out. I follow them out of the room and press the button on the wall outside.

"Holy shit," Sandy says, looking back at Anthony when she walks back in and then at Hunter. "That's messed up, even for me."

"It wasn't like that," Hunter finally says. "It's all his fault." He points at Anthony. "This guy had a hot date," he says and then looks at Sandy, "which I really hope was you and not someone else."

She smiles at him and bats her eyes. "Guilty."

"It was never my intention to lie to you," he tells me and then glares back at Anthony. "Asshole."

"But you did," I point out.

"Why am I the asshole?" Anthony mumbles.

"Yes," Hunter finally says, "I lied to you, but it was supposed to be one blind date, and well, it was supposed to be one freaking drink, then I showed up and you were shitfaced."

"You got shitfaced before your blind date ever got there?" Sandy asks from beside Anthony.

"I wasn't shitfaced!" I yell. "I was two martinis in."

"So almost shitfaced," Anthony says after I take the piece out of his mouth. The glare I give him stops him from talking, and he shakes his head. "Not shitfaced." Then he looks past me to Hunter, pointing at me. "She wasn't shitfaced."

"Then you lost your phone," Hunter says, "and I had no choice but to return it to you. But I swear I wanted to tell you the whole time."

"Look, can we just fix my tooth first, and then we can get something to eat and straighten everything out?" Anthony says, and Hunter just glares at him. "Don't give me that look. I told you to have a drink with her, not two dates."

"Enough!" I yell. "You"—I point at Hunter—"need to go so I can focus. You"—I point at Sandy—"are going to be my assistant if I need anything, and you …"

I point at Anthony. "I'm telling my mom."

"I'll wait outside," Hunter says and walks away before I can argue with him.

"I think he likes you," Anthony says with a smile, but I glare at him. "You really aren't going to tell our moms, are you?" He lies back in the chair. "It's really not fair."

I take a deep breath and look up at the ceiling and say a little prayer. "That was a dick move." I hear Sandy say.

I ignore them for the next forty-five minutes while I work on his tooth that got knocked out. "We need to fit you for a fake tooth,"

I tell him, taking my glasses off and putting them down. "Good news is hopefully the root of the tooth will attach to the bone," I say, getting up and taking off my gloves.

"Phank you," he says, trying to smile and drooling out of the side of his mouth.

"I want you to come back Monday afternoon and get fitted for the fake tooth, and for the love of god, no more aggressive sex this weekend please," I tell them, and they both throw their heads back and laugh.

"Is it done?" I hear Hunter say from outside the room.

"Why is he still here?" I say in a whisper, looking down and releasing a breath I didn't know I was holding.

Anthony laughs, getting up from the chair. "That guy never gives up if he wants something." He puts his hand around Sandy's shoulders. "And from the looks of it, he wants you."

"Yeah, well, I don't want him," I say. Grabbing my

glasses, I walk out and see him leaning against the wall with his feet crossed at the ankles. Why does he have to be so good looking? Why do his lips have to be so perfect? Why do his biceps have to fill out the shirt so well? Why?

"Laney," he says, and I turn to him about to snap.

"Can you just please stop," I tell him, and he stands now. "Just for a second, give me a chance to think." He goes to say something, but I stop him by holding my hand up. "Please." My voice goes softer and lower. "It's just all too much right now. I just …" I shake my head. "I just need to clear my head."

"Fine," he says and looks at Anthony. "Make sure she gets home." He turns and walks by me, stopping next to me, his voice going low. "I'm sorry I lied to you, but I had the best day today," he says and bends his head to kiss my cheek. I don't say anything; I just stand here and let his kiss linger on my cheek.

"What the puck did you do?" Anthony says, and I look at him confused. "He looks like you just kicked his puppy and threw away his kitten."

Sandy laughs from beside him. "That's a vivid picture."

I shake my head. "You guys don't have to stay. I have some work I was putting off that I'm going to finish, and then I'll call an Uber."

"Are you sure?" Sandy says.

"If Hunter finds out I left without driving you home, I'm going to have to order a whole set of new teeth," Anthony says.

"I won't tell him if you don't," I tell him, looking at Sandy. "I'm going to write you a script for painkillers. Once everything starts wearing off, he might be in some pain." She just nods and then looks at Anthony.

"She's fine," she says, and Anthony looks at her. "She just needs to process things, and it's not going to be easy to do it sitting here with the one person whose fault this is," Sandy says.

"This isn't my fault," he says, and Sandy crosses her arms over her chest. "Okay, it might be a little my fault for not being honest with her, but …" She raises her eyebrow, and he stops saying whatever he was going to say and then looks down. "Fine, we'll leave her be, but I swear to god if he finds out …"

"He won't find out," Sandy says. She finally convinces him to leave, and I lock the office front door after them. Going back to my office, I start on the charts I was putting off.

My mind wanders every time I try to write something down. After two hours of staring into space and writing and then erasing everything, I give up, tossing my pen on my desk just as my cell phone rings. I look down and see that it's Mom. I think about not answering, but I know if I don't, she might send out a search party for me.

"Hello?" I say, answering.

"Oh my god, I'm so, so, so sorry," she starts out saying, and I hear her breathing heavily. "Maureen just called me."

"Who is Maureen?" I ask her, confused, leaning back

into the chair.

"Anthony's mother!" she shrieks. "Anthony called her and gave her the heads-up."

"This is your lesson to never set me up again," I tell her, laughing instead of crying. "You are never to set me up again."

"Define never," my mother counters. "I mean, we shouldn't scratch it off the table right away."

"Mom, you set me up with a guy who sent another guy in his place," I point out. "So, it's safe to say that it means I'm never going on another one of your blind dates again. Ever."

"Fine," she finally says, breathing out, "but this isn't my fault."

"It's no one's fault. Let's just chalk it up to one of those funny things we will laugh about in ten years from now," I say, leaning back in my chair.

"Are you sure you're okay?" she asks seriously. "This other boy … He didn't take advantage of you, did he?"

"Mom," I say, laughing, "he is definitely no boy, and no, he didn't. When he got to the Garden, I was two almost three martinis in."

"Oh my god," she says, gasping in shock. "You didn't take advantage of him, did you?"

"Mom!" I shriek. "For heaven's sake."

"No is no, Laney. Male or female," she points out.

"No one took advantage of anyone. He paid the bill and took me to the best Mexican restaurant I've ever been to. I have to take you there soon," I tell her, and we chitchat for the next five minutes about our family brunch tomorrow.

"Okay, I have to go and start preparing. Your aunt Martha is coming, and we all know how bitchy she is," she tells me. I laugh. Since she married Dad, she has hated Aunt Martha. "Last time, I saw her taking her finger and dragging it across the fireplace mantel looking for dust, that hag."

"I'm sure she didn't," I tell her, rolling my eyes.

"She so did," my mother says. "Anyway, I have to go. See you tomorrow and dress to impress."

"NO BLIND DATES, MOM!" I yell, but it doesn't matter since the line beeps. "Fucking hell."

I get up, grab my bag, and walk out of the office, locking the door behind me. The sun has long since gone down, and the night has settled in. I turn to walk down the steps and startle when I see a person sitting on the bottom step. "Hunter?" I ask.

"Do you know the dangers of a single woman walking in the dark in a deserted area?" he asks, standing up.

"I have no idea, but I'm sure you do," I say, crossing my arms across my chest. "I wasn't going to walk anywhere. I was going to sit on the stoop and call for an Uber."

"Every four seconds, a theft happens," he says, standing. With him standing on the bottom step and me standing at the top step, we are at eye level. "Every nineteen seconds, a crime happens."

"Okay, fine," I tell him, but he doesn't stop.

"Every twenty-nine seconds, someone is assaulted,"

he says, leaning forward just a touch more. I smell him, his woodsy smell surrounding me. His eyes, a dark gray now that the sun has gone down. "Every two and a half minutes, a sexual assault occurs."

"Okay," I say, finally throwing my hands up. "Fine!" I shout. "I get it. Stranger danger."

He shakes his head, trying to hide his smile. "I'm sorry," he says softly. "Can we start over? My name is Hunter. I'm rude and condescending."

"You forgot irritating," I tell him, looking down and then back up. "I'm Laney," I say, holding out my hand, but he doesn't take it. Instead, he grabs my face in his hands and leans in close.

"Say my name, Laney." His voice is soft, and my hands go to his waist to stop myself from tilting forward.

"Hunter," I say almost in a whisper, but it sounds more like a question.

"My name may have been a lie," he says, licking his lips. I'm literally holding my breath as he continues. "But nothing we did was a lie. The talk on the beach, the breakfast, the food trucks."

"I left my phone in your car on purpose," I finally tell him the truth. When he walked around the car after we left Guadalupe's, I took my phone out of my purse and slid it between the seats.

His lips curve into a smile, and although I don't know him that well, I know that if the lights were on, his eyes would be sparkling. "I stalked your Facebook and Instagram in the middle of the night," he says, and now, I'm the one who is surprised.

I throw my head back and laugh, his hands dropping and going to my waist. I wrap my hands around his neck, pushing myself forward. "You were smitten with me?"

"Yeah, I guess you can say that," he says, and then the smile leaves his lips, his fingers gripping me. "Today while you held my hand, the only thing I could think about was kissing you. When you took your thumb and put it in your mouth, I wanted to throw you over my shoulder and drag you somewhere no one could see because I wanted to taste you. The only thing I could think about"—his voice goes low—"was tasting you." He doesn't say anything else. He just leans in, and slowly, ever so fucking slowly, his lips meet mine. My arms go limp around his shoulders, and my back arches toward him. My lips part, and his tongue slides in. I moan into his mouth as our tongues slowly twirl. His hands never leave my hips, and when he finally leaves my lips, we are both breathless.

"Do you want to have dinner with me?" he asks, and I just nod as he turns and reaches for my hand. I follow him to the car, and the whole time, the smile never leaves my face.

Chapter Eight

Hunter

When I walked out of the dentist office, I sat in my car and played the whole day over in my head, knowing I fucked up bad.

I started the car and pulled out of her parking lot, but I only made it across the street before my car turned around and went back. This time, I parked across the street from her building. She asked me to leave, but she didn't tell me that I couldn't follow her or make sure she got home safely. I watched the door open and saw Anthony walk out with his arm around Sandy's shoulders and get into Sandy's car. Fury filled me that he left her all alone and didn't make sure she got home okay.

I picked up my phone right away, calling him. "You're sitting across the street, aren't you?" He answers his phone. "Look, she wanted space, and I knew you would be lurking in the shadows so …"

"She hates me," I say, watching the door the whole time. "You owe me."

"I believe I'm paid up in full," he says, laughing.

"How do you think that?" I ask him.

"I saw the way you looked at her. I haven't seen hearts in your eyes before." He laughs, and I roll my eyes. "It suits you."

"I don't have hearts in my eyes," I tell him, hanging up on him and cutting off his laughter.

I stay in the car till the sun goes down. Seeing that her office has no lights on, I get out of my car and walk across the street to sit on her steps. *I'm just going to make sure she's okay*, I keep telling myself. It's just to make sure she's safe.

I wasn't expecting her to come out when she did, and I wasn't expecting her to give me a chance to explain. I wasn't expecting her to agree to have dinner with me. I swung by Five Guys to grab us burgers and then made my way back to her condo. Except when we got there, I got out and opened the trunk to grab a blanket. I handed her the blanket while she looked at me in confusion. With the food in one hand, my other hand grabbed hers, and I walked across the street to the beach. We walked on the dimly lit beach until we were almost at the shore.

"Hold this." I put the bag of takeout in her hands, grabbing the blanket and opening it on the beach. "I know this wasn't what you were expecting, but …" I start to say, and she smiles.

"I love beach picnics," she says, bending down and

unsnapping her shoes. She steps on the blanket and sits down cross-legged. She reaches into the bag and grabs one foil-wrapped burger. "Your number two," she says, handing me my burger and then grabbing her own. She tears the brown bag down the middle and spills the fries on it. We eat as we discuss the food we had today.

"So that was Anthony?" she says, looking at me once she finishes her burger and makes a ball of her wrapper.

"That was Anthony," I tell her. "That was his Tinder date."

"Oh, Sandy is Tinder's best client." She laughs and stretches her legs out in front of her, leaning back on her arms.

"Oh, I don't think so," I say, putting my feet out and crossing them at the ankles. "Anthony takes great pride in swiping left and right."

She laughs, throwing her head back, and I look at her. "Today was an okay day," she says, "minus the whole sex swing fiasco."

"Well, if he hadn't broken his tooth, I would still be trying to figure out how to tell you my real name," I say, looking down and seeing her yawning. "Let's get you home," I say, getting up and grabbing the bag of garbage. She gets up, dusting off her bottom, and then bends to grab the blanket, shaking it and then folding it.

I walk her upstairs, stopping in front of her door. She takes out her keys and turns to me. I lean forward and push her against the door, my hands on either side of her head "Do you want to have lunch tomorrow?" I ask her as I lean closer to her, our faces almost touching.

"I'm having lunch with my family," she says, placing her hands on my chest. I feel the heat seeping through the cotton. "Do you want to come?" she asks breathlessly.

"Sure," I say, and even I don't believe the word that came out of my mouth. But after seeing the smile she gave me when I did, I would do it over and over again. I lean forward, listening to her gasp once and then hold her breath. I lick my lips, looking into her eyes, and then slowly lower my lips to hers. Soft, sweet, perfect. I step back before I take the kiss deeper, before I put my hands on her face and devour her or kick open the door and literally taste every single inch of her.

"Lock up," I tell her, watching her chest rise and fall. She takes her hand holding the keys and places it on the middle of her chest. "Call me later."

I turn to walk away and hear her voice. "You didn't give me your number."

One step down with my hand on the railing, I look at her, smiling. "Check your contacts." I wink at her and walk down the stairs before she sees that my cock is ready to come out and play.

I hear her door slam shut right before I get into the car, so I turn it on and pull out to head to my house. The phone rings, and I press the connect button on the screen. "Hello?"

"Seriously?" Her voice fills the car. "You put yourself under serial killer." She laughs, and I hear cupboards slamming.

"Oh, you figured it out, did you?" I say, laughing, then I hear glasses clink together. "What are you doing?"

"I'm unloading my dishwasher," she says and then stops talking and making noise. "So, listen, about tomorrow, I know that meeting the parents two dates in is crazy, so I will let you off the hook."

"Laney," I say, turning onto my street, "we are two adults dating. It would happen eventually."

"What?" she whispers, and I keep talking so she doesn't say anything else.

"What time is lunch tomorrow?" I ask her, grabbing my phone and switching it over from Bluetooth.

"It's at one," she says, and now I hear her moving around. "I usually get there at noon."

"Okay, so what time should I be at your house?" I ask her, walking into my house, the cool air hitting me.

"Eleven thirty should be good," she says.

"Okay, I'll be there then," I say, walking to the living room and sitting on my couch. "Did you lock up?"

I hear her exhale. "Believe it or not," she starts, "I've been doing okay without you."

I laugh out loud. "Yes, so I've seen."

"Okay, I'm going to let you go now," she says, huffing out. "See you tomorrow."

"Lock up," I tell her, and she disconnects on me. I get up off the couch and head upstairs to repeat exactly what I did yesterday, but this time, when I fall asleep, I sleep the whole night.

So now I'm in my closet the next morning, drinking my coffee as I choose an outfit to wear for when I meet Laney's family. I don't think I've ever done the whole "meet the parents" thing. I mean, maybe I did for prom, but apart from that, I've never ever gone that route. Especially with my family.

I grab my blue chinos with a baby blue button-down shirt, then a brown belt with matching shoes. I roll the cuffs to my elbows and run my hands through the top of my hair, pushing it back. I get in the car and stop at the flower shop on the way. Walking in, I look around at all the different flowers. My eyes stop on a bouquet of white roses.

"How may I help you?" the woman behind the wooden counter asks me.

"Can I have that bouquet over there?" I point at it.

"Those have two dozen roses," she tells me, turning to grab it.

"That should be good," I tell her, handing her my card.

She nods at me and turns to the table behind her to wrap them in clear cellophane. I grab them from her and make my way over to Laney's.

Jogging up the steps to her condo, I knock on the door. When she opens it, my mouth suddenly goes dry. If I thought the pink silky pjs were hot, today she looks like a sex goddess. And she is fully dressed.

She's standing in front of me with the sides of her blond hair tied back today. Wearing an off-the-shoulder long-sleeved loose ruffled one-piece long shirt that goes into a skirt and ends at her mid-thigh. The sleeves are tied at the wrist, and she has a bunch of bracelets on.

My eyes roam down her body, past her killer legs, to a pair of purple feathered shoes that go across her toes and tie around her ankles. "Are those feathers?" I ask, looking at her shoes, and suddenly, I'm thinking of her wearing nothing but those shoes while I nail into her against the wall.

"Are those flowers for me?" she asks with a laugh. I look back up at her and then back at my hand. With a shake of my head, I reach out, giving her the two dozen roses I picked up for her.

"Thank you," she says, grabbing them. She turns and walks to the kitchen and grabs an empty vase, filling it with water. "They smell so good," she says, leaning in and smelling them. I can't do anything but stare at her. She is honestly a natural beauty. She has almost no makeup on, and I love that about her. That I can put my hands on her face without half of it rubbing off on my hands is everything.

"You look beautiful," I finally say to her. She grabs her purse from the counter, stopping in front of me. The smell of citrus fills me, waking my cock up.

"You're not so bad yourself," she tells me, getting on her tippy toes. My hand comes up and cups her neck, bringing her closer. Her smile lights up her blue eyes, and I lean in and kiss her lips. This time, I push it just a bit, and my tongue sneaks out and mingles with hers. "We need to go," she says once I let her go of her lips.

I nod at her, and we walk out holding hands. As I watch her lock the door, I say, "You need an alarm," and I hear her groan. "Do I have to go over the timeline again?" I ask her when we walk down the steps. I walk to the passenger side and open the door for her.

She stops in front of me. "Please, for the love of god, can you tone down the everyone is waiting to get killed or robbed?" she says, kissing my lips and getting in. "It's a good thing you're hot," she says, and I laugh, closing the door. Walking around, I slide in on the driver's side.

"I never said everyone," I tell her, closing my door and starting the car. "I'm saying you need to be aware of the danger lurking around you." I put my sunglasses on and look at her.

"Like I said." She buckles herself in. "Tone down the stranger danger thing in front of my mother please."

"Fine," I tell her. "I take this to mean we are tabling that talk for another time." I turn my back to the door and look at her, and she copies my stance.

"If it will make you shut up, then we will table the crazy talk for another time," she tells me, smiling.

"I get my way again." I wink at her. Asking her for her parents' address, I enter it in the GPS and proceed. I drive to her parents' house while she talks.

"My aunt Martha will be there," she says. "She's married to my father's brother, and she and Mom are like oil and water. The brothers let them be, or, as they say, family is thicker than water. So, it's been an eventful time. Ever since I can remember, they have always butt heads."

"Okay," I say, looking over at her.

"My mother doesn't do well with her, so because we are dating"—she turns to look at me—"you're on her team."

"There are teams?" I ask her. I've never really met

someone else's family before, so I don't know if this is actually a thing. "Do we get jerseys and stuff?"

"No, there are not"—she laughs—"but I'm her daughter. Therefore, I fall on her team, and you are with me, so you get her by default." She claps her hands. "Yay you." She smirks at me. "Aren't you happy you said yes?"

I nod. "Makes sense," I say as we pull up to the house, and I park. "Shit, I should have gotten flowers for your mother." I look over at her.

Laney lets out a laugh. "Oh, you silly, silly man." She shakes her head and reaches out, putting her hand on my leg. "You're showing up to a family lunch on a Sunday," she points out. "Do you know the joy she will be feeling right now?" I shake my head, not sure about any of this. I mean, I know what my mother would be doing—fucking cartwheels. "She'll be planning our wedding before we buckle back in the car."

"No way," I say, pulling open the door and getting out to meet Laney on her side of the street. "You're joking, right?" I ask her, and she shrugs her shoulders at me. I reach for her hand as we walk up the paved driveway to the house. Shrubs line the driveway all the way to the entrance.

It's a two-story house with brown brick. We walk up the four steps to the red front door, and she walks right in. We hear laughter coming from somewhere inside the house. Then I hear a boy yell, "You sank the eight ball."

"I guess my cousin's kids are here. They must be downstairs playing pool." We step into the entryway, and she walks to the left, and we enter what looks like a study. Brown leather couches face a fireplace, and built-in shelves are all around the room. I scan it, finding a couple of family pictures. She walks over to the side where a wooden desk sits, and she puts her purse on it, turning to me and smiling. "Shall we go face the wolves?" She laughs, walking farther into the house. The staircase right in front of us is on the left. A carpet runs down the middle of each step, and family pictures decorate the wall leading upstairs. The pictures all have different frames and range from when Laney was a baby to now.

"Is your room upstairs?" I ask her with a smile, suddenly wanting to know everything about her.

"Yes," she says, pulling me with her, and we walk past the dining room that is already set for our meal. The brown table has white placemats and white dishes ready. I see a hallway leading to the left. "That is the master bedroom." She points at it and then points at an open white door where the voices of the kids are still coming. "That leads to the basement."

We walk into the family room where a huge flat-screen television playing the football game hangs above the fireplace.

"Hey, everyone," Laney says.

A man sitting on the long thick plush couch looks over and smiles. "Hey, cupcake," he says, raising his hand but not getting up.

The other man sitting on the ottoman gets up and comes to her. "Laney," he says softly, coming to her and taking her in his arms. "You look beautiful," he says, kissing her cheek while he holds her arms in his hands.

"Daddy," she says, looking at him, "this is Hunter. Hunter, this is my father, Gary."

I reach my hand out. "Sir, it's a pleasure to meet you."

"Please, call me Gary." He smiles at me. "That is my brother, Norman." He points at the guy who didn't bother getting up.

I walk to him and extend my hand, nodding. "Pleasure to meet you," I say while he shakes my hand and then turns back to the game.

"Go make sure your mother hasn't killed your aunt," Gary says under his breath.

We walk around the couches to the hall that leads to the kitchen. I look around, taking in the biggest kitchen I've ever seen in my life.

The black cabinets are all around the room, and it's shaped like a U. White counters are all around the three walls. A massive white island sits in the middle of the room with a sink on the side of it that faces another sink that sits under a window. A pile of plates sits on one side of the island, and three bread baskets sit next to it.

"Are these clean?" I hear a woman with short curly hair ask, holding open the cupboard door. She is reaching up to grab one, and then brings it out, blowing inside it.

"Martha, everything in my cupboards is clean." I hear a woman say as she takes something out of the oven and puts it on top of the stove. I know right away who Laney's mom is even without her calling Martha's name. She is the same size as Laney in height. Her hair

85

is a bit shorter, but they look so much alike.

"Honey," Gary says, and she turns to look at us and then smiles. She walks to us, taking off the gloves she was wearing to take out the hot dish and placing them on the island.

"Oh, look at you," she says to me, coming to me and hugging me. "You are so handsome." She turns to Martha. "Isn't Laney's boyfriend handsome?" she asks, holding my arm.

I look over at Martha, and she's eyeballing me from head to toe, nodding her head and humming. "Hunter, this is my mother, Corina," Laney says, and I look down at her.

"Ma'am," I say, and she laughs.

"Don't you ma'am me," Corina says. "I will cut a bitch for saying that to me." I roll my lips, trying not to laugh when she turns to Laney. "Is that how you say it? Cut a bitch? Did I use it right?"

"Yeah," she says, rolling her own lips. Shaking her head, she goes over to her aunt Martha and kisses her on her cheek to say hello. "It smells amazing. What did you make?" Laney says, going over to the stove.

"Beef stew," she says. "It's just about ready. I'm just letting it cool down a touch. Why don't we hustle everyone to the table? Martha"—she looks at her sister-in-law—"get the kids from downstairs."

"Where is Rebecca?" Laney asks about her cousin, her daughter.

"Todd took her away for a romantic weekend to celebrate his big promotion at work," Martha says, smiling. She walks to the door and yells downstairs, "The food is ready, come and wash your hands!"

Corina rolls her eyes. "Bitch," she mumbles under her breath quietly. I try not to laugh and stand here taking everything in as two kids who look nine or ten walk in. Both have brown hair and brown eyes and look like twins, but one is taller than the other.

"Hey, Laney," one of the boys says, coming over to her and hugging her. She hugs him and kisses the top of his head as she squeezes him.

"Justin," she says, looking at the one in her arms and at the other one, who is at the sink washing his hands. "This is Hunter," Laney says to them, and they look at me. "That one is Colton," she says.

"Ooohhh, Laney has a boyyyyfriend," Justin says. Laney pushes the kid away, and he looks shocked.

"I changed your diaper when you were a kid, and I have pictures," she says, and he shrugs and walks away, but not before grabbing a piece of bread. She walks to me, and I put my arm around her shoulder, kissing her head.

"Do you really have the pictures on your phone?" I whisper, leaning into her. "You know that is considered child porn."

She rolls her eyes. "I don't have the pictures. I just threaten them." She pushes me and points at me. "And if you start with the laws and all that, I swear to god ..." I smile at her, and I'm about to lean down and kiss her when her mother yells.

"Let's eat!" her mom yells, walking in from the

dining room. "Hunter, can you bring in the bread baskets for me?"

"Sure thing," I say to her, and she turns to Laney.

"Can you grab the white wine from the fridge?" she says, and Laney goes to the fridge, opening it and grabbing two bottles. Going to the counter and walking to the drawers, she takes out the corkscrew. "That's for Martha," she says under her breath, distributing the beef stew into two deep dishes. "If the cork breaks, no biggie." She shrugs, picking up one full bowl and turning to go back into the dining while I follow her. "Put one basket at each end and then one in middle," she orders me, and I see that Norman and Gary are sitting down already.

Gary is at the head of the table, and Norman is beside him. Justin sits beside Norman, and Colton sits on the other side of Gary. "It smells amazing," Norman says, looking at the bowl that she just put down in front of the men.

"Corina," Martha says, coming into the dining room, "I just threw the towel you had in the powder room into the washing machine because it smelled like mildew," she says, and her face goes into a grimace. "So bad."

Corina straightens next to me, and I look down at her hands to see if she has any weapons or anything she can use as a weapon. "Is it the white towel with the squares at the bottom?"

"Yes," she says, going to her seat next to Justin.

"Oh." Corina laughs. "That's your towel that Justin walked in with when he got here." Now it's Corina's turn to grimace. "It might be your washer." She goes to head of the table, placing her hand on the empty chair that she sits in. "You know, now that I think about it, you did smell a bit funny when you walked in."

Martha's face drops, and Justin leans over and smells his grandmother, who looks over at him and pulls her hand back.

"I smell fine," she says when Justin leans over and smells his grandfather on the other side.

"Grandpa smells weird," he says, and Laney finally comes out of the kitchen.

"Here is the wine," she says, placing it in front of Martha and then walking to the other side to place a bottle in front of her father. She must sense something and just looks at everybody. "Are we eating?" she says. Pointing at the chair next to Colton, she says, "You can sit here." I take my chair, and she sits next to me. Her mother comes back into the room with the second bowl of stew.

She sits at the head of the table in the middle of Martha and Laney. "Gary, serve the kids and your brother," Corina says, and when he grabs the bowl next to him, she picks up the bowl in front of her. "Martha, tell me when to stop," she says, scooping her a spoonful. When her bowl is almost full, Martha tells her to stop, then she does the same to Laney, and then Laney does my bowl.

"Can we eat now?" Colton asks, his fingers tapping next to his heaping bowl.

"Yes," Martha says, and we all start to eat. "So"—

NATASHA MADISON

Martha looks up at me mid-chew—"what do you do for work?" I look at her and then look down. I don't say anything when she pipes in again. "Oh, I'm sorry. Do you not work?" she says, almost smirking and ready to look at Corina.

I chuckle a bit. "I work," I say, and suddenly, I feel all eyes on me, and I'm not wrong. Looking up, I see that everyone is looking at me. "I own a security firm," I say.

"Oh," Norman says, "like ADT and all that? I think I see their ads on television."

I shake my head. "No, I mean, I have a private security firm," I say and see his eyebrows pinch together. "We handle public officials when they are in town, or if there is a high-profile celebrity coming into town, we do their detail."

"Do you have a gun?" Colton asks me, his eyes opened big.

"Yes," I answer honestly.

"Do you have it with you?" Justin asks.

"Um." I look at them, and their eyes go big. "No," I lie.

"Have you ever shot someone?" they both ask at the same time, and I just nod.

"I did two tours in the military," I tell them, and I really fucking hope someone changes the subject soon. My leg starts bouncing up and down while I sit at the table.

"Well, we thank you for your service," Corina says, and I just nod, thankful when the conversation moves on to politics. I don't contribute anything but just eat my meal.

I don't say much and just listen. Laney leans over, whispering in my ear, "Do you really have a gun on you?"

I turn and whisper, "If you find it, you can keep it." I wink at her.

She laughs, and she looks at me up and down, using her hand to rub up and down my back. I laugh when I get up to help clear, and she comes over and grabs my waist, rubbing her hand around it. "Not there," I say, laughing, as I walk to the kitchen with the plates. Her mother stands by the sink, rinsing off the dishes and putting them in the dishwasher. "Would you like me to continue?" I ask her, and she just shakes her head and leans closer to me.

"No, because if I'm not doing this, I have to sit at the table with Martha," she says, winking. "I haven't digested my food yet."

I nod my head. "Got it," I say, placing the plates on the counter, then turning to walk away. When I see Laney come back in with plates in her hands, I grab them from her and turn to place them on the counter when I look down and see her trying to feel my ankle. "Not even close."

"Ugh, really?" she says, standing back up, and then she pats my chest. From left to right, shoulder to shoulder, all the way down. "You okay?" she asks when I look at her, and I just nod with a smile as I walk back into the dining room to help clear the table.

By the time we leave her parents' with hugs and promises to do it again soon, she has felt up my whole upper half of my body and both ankles. We get in the car, and I pull away from the curb. "This is killing me," she says, frustrated, slapping her hands down. "Do you have a gun?"

"Yes," I tell her honestly, "and I also have a license to carry it."

"Oh my god," she says with her eyes open and her mouth also. "Is it in your crotch?" she asks with a gasp. "Like near your junk?" she says with her hand as if she is sticking things in the air.

We both laugh as I make my way back to her house. "Do you want to come up for coffee?" she asks me. "I mean, if you aren't busy and don't have any other plans."

"I'd love to," I say, parking the car and getting out. I hold her hand as we walk upstairs, and she unlocks the door. We walk in, and she tosses her purse on the counter. Then she steps into the kitchen.

"Did you really want coffee?" she asks me, and I look at her.

"Was 'do you want coffee' code for 'come upstairs so I can make out with you and see where you keep your gun'?" I joke with her, walking to her.

She puts her hands on her hips. "Um, no," she says, and I raise one eyebrow, looking at her. "Okay, fine, it was, but I wasn't going to make out with you. I was going to spill the coffee on your pants and see when you took them off."

I gasp out, putting both of my hands on my junk. "You were going to burn my dick? What kind of sick monster are you?" I ask her, and she throws her head back and laughs. Her neck calls out to me, and I don't waste an extra second before I pounce on her. She doesn't stand a chance, and when I finally leave her apartment, she makes sure to verify no guns were in my crotch area. I smile the whole time I drive, and I'm even smiling the next day when I walk into work.

Going into my office, I dump my keys and sunglasses and turn on my computer. After I grab the folders, I walk to the kitchen and start making coffee. I open the fridge to take the creamer out and add it to my coffee. Picking my cup up, I take it and head downstairs. The sounds of Rachel's nails on the keyboard lets me know she's already hit the ground running this morning.

"Good morning," I say, smiling, and she looks up at me, smiling and leaning back in her chair.

"Good morning to you, too, Romeo." She snorts when I look at her with a raised eyebrow. "Oh, don't get all coy with me now."

"I have no idea what you're talking about," I say, bringing the hot cup to my lips and burning my tongue with the first sip.

"Oh, okay, this is how you want to play it? Fine," she says. She clicks on a couple of keys, and then I see the big screen change. I'm about to look over when Dante and Brian come into the room.

"Morning," Dante says, and Rachel quickly shushes him.

"As I was saying," she says, looking back at the full screen.

"Gentlemen, I show you evidence number one. Your alarm was on all weekend long, only disarming when you came home to sleep."

"So?" I ask her.

"So, if you can check this out," she says, pressing another couple of buttons. "This is the activity on your house for the past month. You will see the same pattern for Monday through Friday, but Saturday and Sunday are very different. You see for the past month, the only time you set the alarm was when you were going to Whole Foods or to the gym."

I roll my eyes. "I don't shop at Whole Foods," I inform her, and then Dante lets out a laugh when he looks at me with his arms crossed over his chest.

"You got lucky," he says, now clapping his hands.

"What is everyone clapping for?" I hear Anthony say, coming into the room.

"What the fuck happened to you?" Brian asks when Anthony smiles, and you see his missing front tooth.

"Sex swing," he says, going to a chair in the corner, then looks at Rachel. "I have a dentist appointment at two today. Can you make sure you remind me?"

"I'm sorry," Dante says, "a sex swing took out your front tooth?"

"No," he says and then looks at us. "Well, kind of. It was one of those portable ones you hang from a doorframe. You know what I'm talking about, right?" He looks at each of us as we all shake our heads.

"I have no idea what the fuck you're talking about," Dominic says, answering for all of us.

"Anyway, I got on it, and she would climb aboard the pole train, and well, when she was getting closer, it snapped, and since my hands were in the harness, I couldn't block my face, and I fell face first. I'm so lucky it was just my tooth, and I didn't break my nose."

"Your nose looks broken to begin with," Dante says at the same time that Rachel gasps.

"Oh my god," Rachel says, "you think you have heard everything when it comes to you, and then boom, you come in and totally leave me speechless again."

He nods again. "You're welcome." He looks over my shoulder at the screen. "What are we studying?"

"Hunter's alarm pattern," Dante says. "Apparently, it's weird."

"That isn't what I said," Rachel admonishes. "I said it was abnormal behavior."

Dante rolls his eyes. "As I said … weird."

"It's not weird," I snap. "Now, can we please forget it and move along?"

"Wait," Anthony says, "are we talking about you banging my blind date?"

"I didn't bang anyone," I say to them when everyone gasps in shock. "And watch your mouth." I point at him.

"Oh, Hunter has a girlfriend," Rachel says. "Is she cute?"

"I'm not answering this," I say at the same time that Anthony says, "She's fucking hot."

"Hold on a second," Brian says. "She was Anthony's

blind date, and you banged her?" He shakes his head. "Jesus, it's bros before hos."

"She isn't a ho," I say with clenched teeth.

"He's in love," Dante says. "I never thought I would see the day, but …"

"Oh, for fuck's sake, can we stop with the high school gossip and work around here?" I say. Grabbing my coffee and walking up the stairs, I leave the four of them laughing and hollering. As I enter my office, my phone buzzes in my jacket, so I take it out and the smile forms.

Thank you for the rose. Have a great day.

It's from Laney. This morning on the way to work, I stopped by the flower shop and bought her a single rose. I left it on her windshield with a note to have a good day.

I'm about to answer her when I hear Anthony's voice boom out on the intercom speaker. "That, my friend, is the look of love."

I look up at the camera in the corner of my office and give it the finger. "Go fuck yourself," I say and then turn back to answer Laney.

My day can only get better if I get to see you again.

I don't have to wait long before she answers me.

Okay!

Chapter Nine

Laney

"So, what are your plans this weekend?" my dental hygienist, Teressa, asks me when the last patient steps out of the office on Friday afternoon.

"I don't think we have any concrete plans." I smile at her when she turns to put our tools in the disinfector.

She laughs. "Do you think the man who stops at a flower shop every single morning to drop off a rose for you doesn't make plans?" she says, pointing at the small bouquet of roses that I set up in one of the offices.

"Okay, fine." I roll my eyes. "We are going to have a picnic on the beach," I tell her. "We are just waiting to see the weather forecast."

"Oh, that sounds romantic," she says, smiling, and I just nod. "And I heard he's hot AF," she says, closing the door to the sterilizer.

My eyebrows pinch together. "Who told you that?"

"Sandy, when she came in on Monday with her man," she says, and I nod, remembering when he came in.

I shake my head, thinking about how this whole week has been like no other.

Every day I come out and there is a rose on my car with a little note, whether it's him telling me to have a nice day or how much he enjoyed the night before. I always smile, bringing the rose to my nose and smelling the freshness of it. He has been working a couple of days this week, but when he wasn't, we were together. His kisses leave me breathless; his hugs make me feel safe.

"Well, I've never seen you like this," she says and walks out of the room. As I walk into my office, I'm thinking *I've* never seen myself like this before. I've also never felt like this before, and I can't help but think it's a little strange to be feeling so much so soon.

Closing the office and walking to my car, I turn on the radio and make my way home. My phone rings in my hand right before I put it down. "Hello."

"Hey, beautiful." I smile when I hear his voice, and all the thoughts, doubts, and questions just go away. I live in the moment. I want to live in the moment. I don't want to overanalyze whatever this thing is.

"Hey, yourself," I say, the call switching to my Bluetooth as I make my way home.

"Soooo …" He draws out the word. "I was thinking maybe we could have dinner at my place," he says.

"Really?" I say, smiling. "I was wondering if you even had a house or it was a bat cave?"

"Total bat cave," he says, "but Alfred cleaned it up and transformed it."

"Well then, if he went to all that trouble"—I laugh—"how could I say no?"

"I could swing by and pick you up," he says and then his voice goes lower. "Maybe you can spend the night?"

I laugh. "Is this your way of telling me you want to have sex with me?" My stomach's doing somersaults and cartwheels, my vagina suddenly waking up.

"No," he says out loud. "I mean, I'd like to, don't get me wrong, but I just meant that we can have dinner, drink a bit."

It's my turn to get one up on him. "Do you know the dangers of drinking?" I tell him, and he belly laughs.

"Very funny. You can fill me in about all the dangers if you like, but how about I stop by in thirty minutes, and you can tell me?"

"Fine," I agree, "but can it be an hour? I'm not home yet, and I'd like to shower."

"Yup, an hour is good," he says. "See you then. Drive safely."

I rush home and call Sandy while I toss my overnight bag on the bed. I look at it and realize it's the same bag I used to take to Trevor's house, and all of a sudden, I hate it. I take the bag and toss it back in the closet. "Hello there, sunshine," she says, picking up the phone after two rings. "What's shaking?"

I put the phone on speaker while I rummage through the closet for another bag. "How soon is too soon to sleep with someone?" I ask her, and she laughs.

"You're asking the woman who should buy stock in Tinder," she says.

"I haven't had sex since Trevor, and even that was only okay at best," I tell her. "And well, with Hunter, you know that it has to be good."

"Oh," she says, agreeing, "you know that man is packing in the dick area just by the way he walks."

"How does he walk?" I ask her, opening my lingerie drawer, tossing and moving things around, not exactly sure what I'm looking for.

"He walks with the 'my dick is big' walk," she says. "Like with swagger."

I stop, shuffling my underwear around while I try to think if I can remember his walk. "I mean, you've sucked his dick, right?"

"Um, no," I tell her, and she gasps in shock. "Don't even start."

"It's been a week," she says. "If you're not sucking his dick, someone else is."

"Not everyone is as sexual as you are," I point out, thinking I didn't see him every day, so maybe he does have someone else sucking his dick.

"I beg to differ," she says. "Once you get the D, and it rocks your world, you crave it. It's sort of like a drug."

I pick up a pair of black lace panties "Well, what if his D is good," I start, and she hums, "like it's so good that I really want it all the time?"

"Yes," she says, "go on."

"And then we break up?" I say.

"Buzzkill," she says, her laughter making me laugh.

"I haven't really had the D so good that I would think of craving it. Trevor was enjoyable. At least he got things done, but I wouldn't stop watching television to bounce on him."

"Okay, first off, that should have been a sign," she says. "Life is too short for sex to be just enjoyable." She laughs. "I mean, bottom line and worst-case scenario, we sign you up on Tinder."

I shake my head. "Okay, we are getting off topic here." I pick up the pink lace and toss it back into the drawer. "Should I go prepared to have sex, or should I not shave and automatically cross that off the list?"

"Laney, I love you," she starts and huffs out, "but listen to me, and listen to me carefully. You always, always, always shave." She groans, and I smile while she continues talking, and I continue my search to find something sexy. "What if something happens to you in the car? Car crash, trapped inside; we are talking anything where the firemen have to use the jaws of life to pull you out of the car. And with all the turmoil to make sure not to move your neck, they accidentally rip off your skirt or have to cut off your pants because it's stuck on debris. And while doing this, they look down because they are guys, and you know they are looking down when you are so hot looking, and then they do it, and it's like 70's porn down there?" She gasps. "They will be going back to firehouse fifty-one, and chances are none of them will be wondering if you're okay or not because they will be too busy judging your hairy vagina."

I roll my eyes. "You know that *Chicago Fire* isn't real, right? That there is no Kelly Severide, and besides, my vagina isn't hairy. I'm properly groomed," I tell her. "I'm not an old maid virgin, Sandy. I have had sex before."

"I beg to differ," she says. "Anyway, I have to go. Anthony is coming over again, and well, we are going to try to set a record for how long we have sex this time." She squeals. "I can't wait."

"What?" I shriek.

"We're up to six hours. I think we could top it at seven," she says seriously. "It all depends on the positions and the speed. I'm thinking slow and steady." *Is she serious right now?*

"Who the fuck has sex for six hours?" I ask. "Seriously, who?"

"People who get the good D, Laney!" she says, and I hang up on her.

I shuffle things around in my drawer, and my hands land on the black lace one-piece lingerie I bought after I broke up with Trevor. I take it out and hold it up; this would be my 'have reckless sex with someone to get over your cheating closet gay ex-boyfriend' lingerie. "Yes, this is going to be perfect," I say. "You are going to knock his socks off."

I walk to the shower and make sure that everything is cleanly shaven, then I apply my champagne and strawberry body cream and slide into the one-piece black lace and mesh lingerie. I look at myself in the mirror, and I love the way it fits even better than before.

The bra cups are demi, and the wiring under it is pushing them up a touch. Lace covers my stomach all the way down. Turning to check the back, it shows that the back is all mesh and a thong. "It's going down."

I grab a one-piece sleeveless black dress and slip it on. The waist is elastic, so it sucks in, and the top is flowy. I take out my black stilettos and slide them on, tying them around my ankle. I leave my hair down and loose. When I hear him knock on the door, I smile to myself, smooth down my skirt to make sure it's okay, and walk to the door. I'm swinging my hips even if no one is watching. It makes me feel sexy. Or it could be that I know I'm wearing something sexy under my dress. It's surprising how lingerie can make you think you're suddenly a Victoria's Secret model on the runway with the wings.

I swing the door open, and instead of him having his mouth open, I'm the one gaping. He stands there in his black suit that has to be tailor made because it fits him to a T. His white button-down shirt is open at the collar, but it's not just his outfit; it's his stance and just the way he's standing there. Then I go and think about what Sandy said, and my eyes have a mind of their own as they roam down his body, finally arriving at his crotch area. He has to be packing a big D in there. His hair is combed over on top. His jaw is square, and his smile is more of a smirk, but it's his eyes that get me. They are almost crystal clear today.

"Holy shit," he says, stepping forward and wrapping his arm around my waist to bring me closer to him as

I smell him. "You look …" He doesn't finish; he just crashes his lips on mine, and with just one kiss, I melt into his arms. My arms wrap around his neck as I turn my head to the side and deepen the kiss.

"Are you ready to go?" he asks when he finally lets my lips go.

"Yeah, I just have to grab my bag," I tell him and walk to the counter, taking my small clutch bag.

"Is that it?" he asks me, looking down at my hand. The purse only big enough for lipstick and a credit card.

"Yeah, I figure if I'm sleeping over, we are going to be doing it naked." I smirk at him as I walk past him to the door. "So, I don't have to bring anything." His jaw goes tight, the vein in his forehead bulging, and now I see how fast his eyes have changed from crystal to shaded.

He turns and walks to me, grabbing my hand and taking the key from the other hand while he locks the door. He doesn't say anything to me when he leads me to the car, closing the door after I slide in. So, I just look out the window and smile.

When we pull up to his house, I take in the houses that are side by side. The gray brick doesn't really give it away except you see four windows, two on the top and two on the bottom. I get out of the car and wait for Hunter to meet me. "Welcome to my home." He smiles.

Grabbing my hand, he walks me to his black front door. Using his thumb, he unlocks it. "Oh, that's interesting," I say, "for me to rob you, I have to cut off your finger." I nod, smiling. "Good to know." He pushes the door open, and I step in and stop in my tracks. I just stare because there are no lights on in the house, but you don't need any lights because his whole back wall is windows, and all I can see is endless ocean.

"Come on," he says with a smile, walking around me and pulling me in. The floor plan is completely open, so you see his dining room, living room, and kitchen.

The wall to the right is an all-white brick with the stairs leading to two doors upstairs. The railing is all glass. "This is breathtaking," I say to him, putting my purse down on the table by the door.

"Oh, you haven't seen anything yet," he says, picking up a remote. He presses a button, and the whole wall of windows slowly opens, showing you the patio outside. The sound of waves is now filling the house. "Come with me." He extends his hand to me. I grab it, our fingers linking together, and we walk outside to the deck or at least one of them.

There are three separate areas. The outside table is under what is an awning or looks like an awning, but when I walk more into the middle of the deck, I see it's a balcony from upstairs. I look upstairs and see another deck, where I spot a hot tub and sitting area.

To my left is five steps up with a sun tanning section with two lounge chairs facing the beach, and then to my left three steps down is a sofa set. "This is almost like a vacation home," I tell him, and he just puts his hands in his pockets and shrugs.

"I worked hard, so I thought why not splurge a little," he tells me, and I just nod my head. "Do you want to eat out here?"

he asks me, and I just smile, nodding. "I'll get you something to drink," he says, going back inside. I watch him as he shrugs his jacket off and tosses it on a stool at the counter. He rolls up his sleeves and makes his way behind the counter. I turn back to look at the ocean and walk down the steps to the L-shaped outside sofa and sit down. The ottoman in the middle has two lanterns that are turned on. I watch the waves crash into the shore, waiting for him to come back, and when he does, it's with two margaritas in his hands. He hands me the one with the lemon in it. "This one is yours."

"Oh my gosh," I say, grabbing the glass. "You have big shoes to fill. I haven't gotten the taste of Guadalupe's out of my head since last week."

"Well, then I will say that she made these for me," he tells me, and I look at him shocked. "Today is one week from our first date." He sits next to me. "So, I went by her place, and she made me the same thing we had last week."

"What?" I say, shocked, thinking no one has ever done anything this sweet.

"Happy one week," he says, holding up his margarita glass, no doubt with no tequila in it, even if he isn't driving. I raise my hand and smile at him. As I look into his eyes, he clicks his glass with mine but kisses me on the lips before I can even sip it. Once I bring the glass to my lips, the salt immediately hits my tongue and the tangy bite of lemon completes it.

I drink half of it and then look at the ocean. "I don't

think I would go anywhere if I lived here," I tell him as I curl my feet under me, and he leans back on the couch, his arm slinging over my legs.

"It's funny, but I rarely get out here," he says, "I'm just so busy that I never really take the time to enjoy it, I guess."

"Well, then it's a good thing we met," I tell him, leaning over to kiss him. His lips taste like lemon.

We hear a timer go off in the house; his hand comes up and cups my face, his thumb rubbing my wet lips now. "That's the queso," he says, getting up. "Do you need any help?" I ask him, leaning forward, ready to get up, but he just shakes his head.

"I need you to sit here and enjoy the view," he says, leaning down to kiss me gently on the lips and then walking away. I watch the way his ass is a perfect fit in his black pants.

"Oh, I'm definitely enjoying the view right now," I say, and he stops in his tracks to look over his shoulder at me. I bring my margarita to my mouth to hide my smile. Then place it down again looking at him.

"That mouth is going to get you in trouble tonight," he says, and I know it's not an empty threat.

"Promises, promises," I say with a smile, bringing the margarita back to my lips to finish it off while he turns and walks into the house.

He comes back out with a tray and sets it down in the middle of the table. "We have queso and guac," he says, "and I brought you another margarita and water."

I laugh. "I'll have some water," I tell him. I don't

want to be blitzed the first time we have sex. Holy shit, we are actually going to have sex. But what if he doesn't want to have sex with me?

I grab a chip and dip it in the queso. "I have to say, this might be even better than last week."

"Really?" he says, tasting it. "It tastes the same as it does all the time," he says, looking at me.

"Yeah," I agree with him and then add, "except last week, I was out with a broody jerk. But now I'm sitting with a man who gives me butterflies," I say, shrugging one shoulder outward and smiling shyly.

"Butterflies?" He smirks at me, leaning back again and draping his arm across my legs tucked under me.

"Well, you are dreamy," I tell him, moving one finger in an S across his bare arm. "You're still irritating." I laugh when his eyebrows shoot together. "With your lists and all."

He shakes his head. "I'm trying to keep you safe," he says seriously. "There is so much danger that you don't know about."

I close my eyes, listening to him go on. "Do you have sex often?" I interrupt him, and I open my eyes.

"What?" he asks as if he's not sure he heard me right.

"Do you have sex often?" I ask the question again. "Like have you had sex in the past week we've been together?"

"One, I don't have sex that often, and two, I definitely haven't had sex in the past week." He turns to look at me. "Have you?"

"No!" I shriek. "Of course not. But someone told me

that if I'm not sucking your dick, then someone else is. So …"

He sits up, handing me a water bottle. "Drink water," he says, "lots of it."

"I'm not drunk, you ass. I'm trying to have a conversation with you." I put my margarita glass down, taking one leg out from under me.

"A conversation about someone sucking my dick?" he points out.

"NO!" I say loudly and then turn, looking at him. "I've had sex; you've had sex"—I point at him and then me—"but we haven't had sex with each other." I hold out my hands. "So, I thought we could talk about it before actually doing the deed."

He throws his head back and laughs. "Baby, when we have sex, there will be no talking about it." He leans into my space now, his hands cupping my face. "I also don't want to talk about anyone you've had sex with." Gone is his smile, and in its place is a man who looks ready to snap.

"It's just …" I start, and he just shakes his head.

"No, it's just nothing, Laney," he says, grabbing me and dragging me to him. I am now straddling him on the couch. He groans when my pussy lines up on his dick.

The clothes between us are suddenly too much. He pushes my hair away from my face. "I've never had a girlfriend," he starts. "I've had sex." Shaking his head, he says, "Which we aren't going to discuss now or ever. This with you and me came out of the blue and knocked me on my ass."

"Really?" I ask, my hands now going up his chest to the collar of his shirt while I run a finger inside his shirt along his collarbone.

"Really," he says. "I didn't invite you here tonight expecting sex." I start to say something, but he puts his finger to my mouth. "I'm not saying I don't want to have sex with you. I'm saying that it wasn't my intention."

"Bu—" I say, and he shuts me up again.

"But if it happens, I'll be one happy son of a bitch," he says, and I laugh. "So how about we go inside, get our tacos, and eat?"

He takes his finger off my mouth. "How about," I say, "you show me upstairs first, and then we can have tacos later?" I get off him and hold my hand out to him. "Like much, much later." He raises his eyebrow at me while he looks at my hand and then my face. "Show me upstairs, Hunter."

He grabs my hand, and we walk inside. Neither of us says anything as we walk up the stairs. He presses something on the keypad by the light switch, and I hear the windows downstairs start closing.

I look inside one of the two doors, and he leads me to the one on the left. I gasp when I see his bedroom because it isn't two rooms; it's one huge room.

To the left is a beige couch that faces the television on the wall above the fireplace. Throw pillows decorate each end and a plush beige blanket is thrown over the back of the couch. The middle ottoman is the same fabric. But then to the right is the bedroom part.

His huge king-size bed is in the middle of the room

with a beige and dark brown headboard. As I walk into the bedroom, my feet sink into the plush white carpet. I look up and see that he has six windows on his ceiling, showing you the sky.

His white duvet looks like a cloud. I walk past it, dragging my hand on it while I walk to the wall of windows. The doors open, and I look back at him. "It's a motion thing."

I shake my head, laughing. "This is like a secret hideaway."

"Almost," he says, leaning against the doorframe, his feet crossed at the ankle. He touches the light switch, which dims the lights in the room, and I see that a light is coming from the living area and then lights come from behind his headboard. "You look like an angel standing in the middle of the room with the lighting like this."

I cross my arms in front of me. My hands go to the elastic in the dress, and I peel it over my head, tossing it to the side. I watch him as he now stands straight. "Do I still look like an angel?" I ask him and turn in a circle so he can see all of me. I don't have time to do a full circle before I feel him at my back.

"Last chance," he says between clenched teeth, and I don't say anything to him. Instead, I get on my tippy toes and wiggle my ass on him, leaning back and wrapping one hand around his neck.

"You're wearing too many clothes," I tell him, and his mouth crashes against mine.

Chapter Ten

Hunter

She's standing in the middle of my bedroom wearing fucking black lace, and the only thing I can think of is tasting her, worshiping her, claiming her, and making her mine. All. Fucking. Mine.

I approach her from behind, and my hands go to her hips when all I want is to cup her tits in my hands. "You're wearing too many clothes," she whispers seductively as her hand moves to my neck. I snap, crashing my mouth down on hers.

My tongue slides into her mouth, and I taste salt and citrus. I groan, and my hands roam from her hips to her tits as I cup them in my hands. Her ass moves against my cock, and I'm now rock fucking hard. The kiss goes from soft to needy as she turns around, and our mouths never leave each other. I grab her, and she wraps her legs around my waist as I carry her to the bed.

I put my knee on the bed and slowly drop her on her back. I let go of her lips as her chest rises and falls. Her hair spreads out on the bed. Her legs fall from my waist as I stand between them. I lean forward when I see one of her nipples pebbled and half out, and using my tongue, I go under the lace and around the nipple, sucking it deep into my mouth. Her back arches up as I do the same thing with the other nipple. I then lean back and take the shirt out of my pants while she watches me. Her legs open, and I see that she's already wet through her lace.

I unbutton my shirt and take it off, showing her my chest. She sits up. "Holy shit," she says, touching the muscle at the side of my hip. "I thought this V muscle was a myth."

I laugh at her. "Lie back down," I tell her, and she does. I unbuckle my pants and let them fall to the floor. I stand here in front of her in my black Hugo Boss boxer briefs, my cock pushing against the fabric to get out. I crawl onto the bed, pushing her legs apart. Her breath comes out in a soft gasp. I push her legs back and get down between her legs. She's open to me. The only thing between my mouth and her pussy is lace. "Fuck," I say and use my tongue to lick up her slit. One of her hands flies to my head. I do it again and again till the lace is soaked with her juices. I take my hand and move the lace aside, and her pussy is now open for me. "I'm going to make you come with my mouth and then with my cock," I tell her, leaning down and teasing her clit. I suck it into my mouth at the same time as I slide a finger in her.

Her back arches up, and her legs squeeze my head. I finger her while teasing her clit, and I know when she comes because her pussy squeezes my finger as she spasms around my finger. I finger her till she is limp on my bed, then pull my finger out and get off the bed to go to the bedside table. "I need to thank Anthony for the housewarming gift," I tell her, grabbing the box of condoms and climbing back on the bed. She props herself up on her elbow and looks at me, the pink tint in her cheeks.

"I didn't even see you naked," she says, and I peel my boxers down my legs. "Holy shit, you do have a big dick."

I close my eyes. "What?"

"Sandy said you have to have a big D because of the way you walk."

"I'm not even going to discuss this right now," I say, opening the condom wrapper with my teeth. I watch her get up on her knees and peel the one-piece off. Lying down, she throws it right next to my feet. She's finally naked in front of me, and she's stunning. She's perfect, lying in the middle of the bed, and I go to her, my eyes on her the whole time. I roll the condom down my cock, taking him in my hand, her legs open wider for me. I rub my cock up and down her slit—once, twice, three times—and then slowly slide into her. I lean forward once I'm balls deep and take her mouth.

I twirl my tongue with hers as I fuck her slowly; so slowly, I think I'm going to kill myself before her. She's so fucking snug. She lets go of my mouth to toss her head back and moan. I watch myself disappear inside her, her body taking me, all of me. Her hand goes to the back of my neck, and I lean forward, sucking her neck. "Harder," she says, and I know she's at the edge. I go all out, and this time, I pound her hard—still slow but hard. She meets me with every single thrust, and finally, she goes over the edge and comes on my cock. I wait for her till I can't breathe anymore and finally plant myself inside her and come, groaning into her neck. I try not to crush her, rolling to my side and bringing her with me, my cock still inside her. I try to catch my breath, and she gives my chest little kisses. "Hmm." She moans as she continues kissing me, and my dick never gets a chance to go down. I pull out of her as she groans in protest and then I take off the condom. "Come back," she says, closing her eyes, and I watch her on the bed with a hand between her legs.

"You playing with yourself, waiting for me?" I ask, getting another condom. She opens her eyes and watches me. I roll the condom on, then get on the bed. She pushes me on my back and then climbs on top.

We spend four hours having sex, doing it over and over and over again. "I can't move," she says, lying on her stomach, "but I'm starving."

"I'll go warm up the food and bring it to you," I tell her, getting up and putting my boxers on.

"I get it," she says, her voice muffled in the pillow. "I'm totally addict to the D."

I look at her and laugh. "I really hope just my D and

not someone else's."

She laughs, raising her head off the pillow and turning onto her side. "Definitely yours."

"Good to know," I say, walking out of the room. A second later, I hear her feet following me. "I thought you couldn't move?" I ask her when she walks down the stairs, her hair piled on her head, wearing my white button-down shirt.

"I don't want to eat in bed and get crumbs everywhere," she says, coming to the kitchen and sitting on a stool as I warm up the taco stuff.

"My body feels like I just ran a marathon," she says, stretching her arms over her head. "I mean, if marathons were that much fun, I'd be the fittest person ever."

I laugh to myself. "Why do you make me laugh so much? I don't think I've ever laughed this much," I tell her, thinking how different and refreshing this feels.

I put the plate of tacos on the island and grab a stool to sit in front of her. "Holy shit," she says, chewing, "these are so good."

I nod while I chew. "No one does Mexican like Guadalupe," I say.

"Do you still want to have a picnic this weekend?" she asks me as she takes another bite.

"Yeah, if you want," I say, chewing my second bite.

"Or," she says, grabbing a water bottle and drinking some, "we could just camp out here and picnic on your beach." She winks at me. "Just a thought."

"I like that thought a lot," I say, finishing my taco.

We finish eating and clean up before I set the alarm,

and then we walk up the stairs hand in hand. "We should take a shower," she says, walking into the room, "together. You know, to preserve water."

"Obviously," I tell her, leading her to the bathroom and turning on all the lights. She stops at the doorway and takes in the bathroom. Okay, fine, I might have gone overboard. The white room is beige, lights set in the molding in the ceiling. The shower is all beige with five recessed lights and twelve showerheads, and the whole thing is surrounded by glass, showing you the L-shaped bench.

"Oh my god," she says, walking into the bathroom and looking around. "I changed my mind. Let's have a picnic in here." She walks toward the elevated bathtub. One step up and you will see the sunken tub that sits right in front of a fireplace in the wall.

She approaches the shower where I open the door and set the temperature. "Your shower is the size of my closet," she says, slipping the shirt off and stepping in. "Actually, it's the size of my bedroom *and* closet," she says, and I follow her. "Is the bench heated?" she asks me, and I just nod my head.

"Yeah, why?" I answer her, going to the wall and pressing the button.

"I want it to be warm when I have you sit down and ride you." She winks at me over her shoulder. I walk to her, turning her around and pushing her back toward the bench. The back of her knees hits it first, and she uses her hands to sit down.

"Is it warm?" I ask her as she sits down.

"Yes," she says.

"Are you comfortable?" I ask her, and when she nods, I get down on my knees in front of her. "I want you to be really, really comfortable."

"I'm comfortable," she says softly. I see her chest rising and falling, my hands coming up to pinch her perfectly pebbled nipples. Water drops trickle down her chest, and I push her softly till her shoulders are leaning on the back wall.

"I want you as comfortable as possible because," I say, leaning forward and taking her nipple in my mouth, "I'm about to have my dessert." Her breath hitches. I kiss her chest and slowly give her kisses till I get to her belly button. "I have to say, I saved my appetite for this right here," I say, pushing her knees apart. "I think I see exactly what I want to eat," I say, winking at her right before I bury my face between her legs. Her moans fill the shower, her knees opening even wider, and her hand grabs my hair as she pushes me deeper in her. I savor her till she comes on my tongue. Both of us take what we want from each other, and by the time we finally collapse in bed, I think the sun is coming up.

"What is that noise?" I hear mumbled from beside me as I sit up right away. "Stop the ringing."

Looking around the room, I find the source of the ringing coming from my pants. I get out of bed, take it out of my pants, and leave the room so I don't wake up Laney.

"Hello," I say, and I hear Anthony's voice, which is just as groggy as mine, and he's whispering also.

"We have a situation," he says, and I'm already alert and ready. All sleep is gone from me the minute I hear those four words.

"The package we delivered last month wants to come back and visit," he says, and I turn to stare at the door, making sure that I'm still alone.

"Are you saying that Kelly Taylor is coming back? Why didn't her people call us yesterday?" I ask him. Kelly is the biggest name in music. She is known to jump from guy to guy, but she wants to keep her latest romantic conquest quiet, so she comes to town and we sneak her around.

"She called me herself," he says. "Coming on a private jet, arriving at three this afternoon. She'll come straight to our office."

"Okay," I tell him. "I'll meet you at the office at two, and we can go over a plan at the office."

"See you then," he says, hanging up the phone. I walk back into the room and see Laney in the middle of the bed on her stomach with the sheet to her neck. I smile as I head to my closet, slipping on my shorts and going downstairs to start the coffee. Grabbing my iPad, I walk back upstairs and see she hasn't moved, so I walk to the living room side and the door opens right when I stand in front of it. I walk out onto the patio after putting my iPad on the couch and look out at the beach. Families have set up for the day, and the runners are already pounding up and down the beach. I look up and don't see a cloud in sight, so it's going to be a hot one. I turn and go to sit on the couch, picking up my iPad and coffee.

I scroll through the news on CNN and Fox, check my stocks, and look at some of the cases coming up in the next couple of weeks. It's going to start to get busy; the music festival is going to kill us because they just added three more headliners, and the first daughter is coming to town also. "There you are." I hear from the bedroom part as Laney walks out wearing my robe. "I was looking for you," she says, walking to me and rubbing the sleep from her eyes.

"I got a phone call about work, and I didn't go back to bed," I tell her and hold out my arm to her. She comes and sits on my lap and leans back on me, kissing my neck. "Morning," I say softly as I hug her, and we watch the water. I sit here, completely content with everything for once. My mind's on work, but it's not pushing me to get off the couch, and it's not playing over and over in my mind. Instead, I live in this moment right here.

"Do you want me to make breakfast?" she asks from my neck, kissing me again.

"Sure," I say to her. She gets off my lap, and we make our way downstairs. "I made myself a coffee when I woke up before; do you want me to make you one?"

"Yes, please," she says and pins her hair up on top of her head.

I lean over and kiss her lips, bringing my hand to her face. "I love when you tie your hair," I tell her. "It makes it easy for me to do this." I lean in, biting her neck and then kissing it. "How do you take your coffee?"

"Just black," she answers me, and I turn to start her coffee with the Keurig. "How do you like your eggs?" she asks me, going to the fridge to open it and look inside. "We got some turkey bacon, regular bacon, some sausage." She looks up from the fridge. "Someone really expected a sleepover," she says, laughing.

I shrug. "I was hoping anyway."

"How do you want your eggs?" she says, opening the cupboard till she finds what she's looking for and pulls out a frying pan. She places it on the burner and then goes to the drawers for a spatula.

"I don't really have a preference as long as they're cooked." She grabs the bacon, then turns and gets things started. I sit at the island, watching her make me breakfast. "I could get used to this."

"What?" she asks, turning to look at me as she scrambles the eggs.

"You cooking for me." I smirk at her.

"I owe you," she says, shrugging.

"For what?" I ask her.

"For about twelve orgasms last night," she says, smiling. "And for the visit down under," she says, pointing the spatula to her vagina. "Gives new meaning to thunder down under."

I laugh at her. "Good to know, and by the way"—I pick up my own coffee, bringing it to my lips—"fourteen," I say, "but hey, who's counting."

"I'm pretty sure it was twelve," she says, looking up and counting. I see her moving her lips as she counts and then her fingers. "Yup, fourteen."

"See," I tell her with a wink. I'm about to take a drink of my coffee when my phone starts ringing. I look down at it, see it's Anthony, and then I look up at her again as she watches me.

"I'll be right back," I say, grabbing the phone and walking outside to the back deck.

"Hey, it's me. Change of plans. She got an earlier flight."

"What?" I ask. "How is that possible?"

"Well, when you have a private jet at your disposal, you don't have to really wait. Meet me in ninety," he says.

"Fuck, fine. I'll be there as soon as I can," I say, disconnect, and then look inside at Laney who is still cooking. I walk back in, and she looks at me.

"Is everything okay?" she asks, and I look down and then up again.

"Yeah, it's just a change of plans actually. I have to go. It shouldn't take long, and we can meet up after," I say to her and something in her eyes changes, but I can't pinpoint it.

She puts the spatula down. "Oh, yeah. I'm sorry." She shakes her head. "I'll get out of your way." She puts all the eggs on a plate and then looks at me, giving me a fake as fuck smile. "Yeah, okay. I have stuff to do at home anyway."

I walk to the island, and she puts the plate of eggs in front of me and then turns to me. I notice the change in her right away.

"Eat." She smiles, pointing at the eggs. "I'm going to go and shower, and then I can get an Uber." She walks to the stairs almost as if she's running to get out of here.

"Like fuck you will," I tell her, and she stops on the steps, looking over at me and then away. "I'll drive you home."

She just walks upstairs, and I hear the shower turn on. I don't bother even eating the food. Instead, I go upstairs, taking the steps two at a time. I walk into the bedroom to the bathroom, and seeing that the door is closed, I reach out to turn the handle and find it locked. "What just happened?" I ask myself and then go to sit on the bed with my phone in my hand. My leg starts moving up and down, and the water finally turns off. I don't have to wait long before she comes out of the bathroom fully dressed. Her hair is still piled on the top of her head. "Is something going on?" I ask her, and she just shakes her head.

"I'm just tired," she says and then looks at me. "I'm going to go get my shoes outside." She walks out of the room and heads downstairs. I look at the time and curse that I have to fucking go, which means I can't stay here and find out what the hell just fucking happened.

I grab some jeans, a T-shirt, and my running shoes. I walk down the stairs, and I know even before my foot hits the living room floor that she isn't here. "Laney." I call her name, and she isn't anywhere. I look outside and then see the paper on the table under the lantern.

Hey, didn't want to bother you. Thanks for last night. See you around.

"See you around? What the fuck is this?" I say and pick up my phone to call her, but she sends me straight to voice mail. I wait for her beep before talking, and when I do, it's with clenched teeth.

"Laney, you better have a good excuse for ditching me and walking out and not saying anything. I'll be at your house as soon as I can," I say and then stop for a second. "Please call me." My voice goes soft at the end, and I toss my phone on the couch and sit down, running my hands through my hair. I get up, grab my keys and sunglasses, and head out, the only thing running through my head is going to see Laney.

Chapter Eleven

Laney

When I walked out of the bathroom and saw him sitting on the bed, I was almost tempted to go to him, but I didn't. I made a run for it. I ran out to get my shoes, and luckily, the Uber driver was waiting for me. I knew I was only getting a couple of minutes head start, but the faster I got away from him, the better my head would feel. The blurriness of the truth would be there.

When my phone rings four minutes later, it doesn't take a rocket scientist to know who it could be. I look down and see his name pop up "serial killer," but my finger doesn't linger over the green button before pressing the red one right away. I send him straight to voice mail as I look out the window. My phone rings again, and this time, it's Sandy.

"Hello," I answer right away.

"Where are you?" she whispers.

"I'm in an Uber, why?" I tell her and then ask, "Why are you whispering?"

"I'm," she says, "I'm hiding in Anthony's bathroom."

"Is he home?" I ask, all confused.

"Yes," she says, "but I think he's going on a date with someone else."

"What?" Now, I'm really confused. "Aren't you at his house at this moment?" Then I hear Anthony in the background yell her name. "Oh my god, does he know you're even there?"

"Hey," she says in a normal voice. "Are you leaving?" She must ask him, and I hear him tell her that he will be back as soon as he can. "Okay, bye."

"That motherfucker," she says, coming back on the phone, and I hear her rushing around the room. "He thinks he can cheat on me."

"Sandy!" I yell, "What the hell are you talking about?"

"I can't talk now. I have to go follow him."

I roll my eyes. "Oh, Jesus, woman, can you calm down before you go off half-cocked?"

"I will not calm down," she says, and I hear the car door slam, and the tires squeal. "I have to go. I have to see where he is."

"How are you going to do that?" I ask her.

"I put a tracker on his phone," she tells me, and I shriek.

"Are you crazy?"

"I don't even know why you would ask me this question. You know me. Of course, I'm crazy. You act like this is news to you."

"Okay, listen to me. I'm going to go home and then come to you. Please, please for the love of god, don't do anything that will get you arrested again."

"That was not my fault!" she yells. "That cyclist didn't obey her stop sign. How was I supposed to know I would hit her?" I put my hand on my forehead, thinking of the time I got a phone call to come bail her out. Not only did she hit the cyclist, but she then also kicked her bike.

"Whatever. Can you just calm down?"

"I can't guarantee anything," she says, disconnecting. As soon as the Uber pulls up in front of my condo, I run inside to grab my car keys and then call her back.

"Where are you?" I ask her, getting into the car.

"I'm parked in front of a townhouse. He was already inside when I got here, then a lady got here with a big hat and glasses. She kept her head down when she walked in."

"Oh my god," I say, mapping her location. "I should be there in seven minutes. Whatever you do, don't get out of the car."

I hang up and rush over there, making it in five. I park behind her across the street from the townhouse. I get out, walking to her car, and see her crouched down in the driver's seat using binoculars. "Sandy," I say, and she turns and yelps.

"Get down," she says. "I don't want him to see you." I stay crouched down and get into the passenger seat. She looks over at me confused. "You came to a stakeout in a dress and heels?"

"I was on my way home from my date when you called," I tell her, and she smiles at me.

"You got the D, didn't you?" she asks, and I roll my eyes. "Was he as big as I told you he was? I bet he was."

"I'm not discussing this with you," I tell her, and then we hear a voice, and she looks out, and I'm shocked for her. Anthony is coming out of the house, and he's holding hands with a woman with a big straw hat and glasses. "Oh, fuck no." I hear Sandy say as she storms out of the car, not giving me a second to think of the next step before she's in the middle of the street yelling.

"You cheating motherfucker!" she yells across the street, and Anthony and the woman stop in their tracks. Anthony's face shows complete shock. I get out of the car and run across the street while Anthony puts his hands up.

"What are you doing here?" he asks her, and Sandy tries to go around him to the woman—to snatch the hat off her head, no doubt—but Anthony protects her, which infuriates Sandy even more.

"You're protecting her?" Sandy yells. "You're protecting that bitch?"

"Excuse me," the woman says. I finally look over at her, and she looks familiar, but I don't think of it anymore. I walk to Sandy, grabbing her arm.

"Sandy," I say to her, hoping I get through to her.

"This ..." she says, now bouncing on her feet, knocking my hand off her. "This woman is who you're cheating on me with?" She points at her. "Miss big hat and sunglasses, it's fucking cloudy, bitch," she says, and the woman puts her hand on her hips.

"I am not cheating on you," he says again and again, and I look behind him and see Hunter coming out of the house.

"What is going on out here?" he says and then looks at everyone and stops at me. "Laney, what are you doing here?"

"She's here with me," Sandy says to him and then looks at Anthony. "I followed this two-timing scumbag here. And what is this, a threesome?"

"I told you before. I'm not cheating on you," Anthony says again, grabbing her arms in his hands.

"Liar!" Sandy yells. "You're a liar."

"I swear to Christ, woman, I am not cheating on you," he says, shaking his head and then bending to look into her eyes, his voice going soft, "I swear to you, baby. I am not cheating on you."

"Then why didn't you want me to suck your dick this morning, eh?" she asks him, shaking his hands off her arms, and I open my mouth. "Last night, we only had sex for two hours," she says, looking at me. "Two."

"Holy shit," the woman says, and Sandy turns to glare at her.

"Yeah, bitch, our longest was six hours," Sandy says, folding her arms over her chest, proud of that fact. "Bet you can't top that? Can you?"

"Enough!" Hunter yells, and then Anthony cuts in.

"I didn't want you to blow me this morning because I'm pretty sure my dick has no more skin left on it," he says, throwing his hands up.

I roll my lips together before I laugh, and Sandy uncrosses her arms and looks at him. "What?" she asks softly.

"My dick is raw, baby," he tells her while she goes to him and touches his hand. "Honestly, we've had more sex than I thought was humanly possible."

I roll my eyes, and the woman standing there puts her hand to her mouth. "I'm dry, baby," he tells her, taking her in his arms. "There is honestly not a drop of fluid left in me. Hulkster needs a rest."

"Okay," Hunter finally says. "That is more information than we need to know," he says, then looks at the woman. "Kelly, I'm really sorry about all this."

"It's okay," she says, smiling, then looks at Anthony. "Six hours?"

"Watch it," Sandy says at the same time it comes to me.

"You're Kelly Taylor." I point at her, and Sandy's mouth opens in shock and then jumps up and down.

"Holy shit. Holy shit, holy shit," Sandy says, laughing.

"I am," she says and then looks at Hunter and Anthony. "Think you can get me to my guy now, so we can try to beat six hours?"

"Anthony, take Kelly," Hunter says, then turns to Sandy. "You meet him later. You," he says, pointing at me, "in my office."

"Excuse me?" I say, crossing my arms over my chest, and I don't think it was the right thing to say to him.

He looks mad, and the vein in his forehead has its own heartbeat.

"How can you be so reckless?" he says, putting his hands on his hips, and the three people stop and look at us.

"Be so reckless?" I ask him. "I was coming to make sure Sandy was okay and wasn't going to be arrested for beating up someone."

"So, you thought by putting yourself in danger, that would be better?" he asks me, and I stop and look at him.

"By helping my friend. Yes, I thought it was a great idea."

He shakes his head. "Well, putting your friend before yourself is …" He laughs bitterly

"Is what, Hunter?" I ask him.

"It's stupid," he says, lifting his hands up to the air. "It's stupid, and it's reckless and childish, and you could have gotten yourself fucking killed." He yells out the last line.

"Hunter," Anthony says, and he shakes his head.

"She didn't even think before she got out of the car. She thinks she's fucking invincible," he says, his voice going higher.

"I got out of the car to help my friend," I tell him.

"Yeah, and what if she had a gun and shot you? How much help would you be? Do you know the shit that I see, that one little action can sometimes take someone's life in the blink of an eye?" he asks, shaking his head. "Stupid." His voice is low like he's talking to himself.

"Running out here like nothing can stop her." I stop listening to him, then I hear him ask me, "How would you have stopped a bullet?" And the only thing running through my head is that he thinks I'm a child and that my actions are reckless.

"Well, you will never know now, will you?" I tell him, and he just stares at me. Sandy comes over and holds my hand.

"You're a moron," she tells Hunter. "She is the most loyal person I have ever met, and she came here to help and protect me."

I shake my head. "It's okay, Sandy. I was just leaving. I wouldn't want to do something stupid or childish while I stand here, defending my reckless behavior," I say, turning to her. "Call me later."

I turn and walk to the car, the whole time hoping that he calls out my name, the whole time trying not to be sad that this thing is over. I've known him one week. We've been together one night, so this is nothing. I've survived worse. I get in the car, pulling away from the curb, and don't make eye contact with anyone, knowing the four of them are watching me. I drive home, the whole time trying not to think about what just happened. I try not to think that this morning when I woke up, I could have honestly said it was one of the best nights of my life. But in the blink of an eye, it came crashing down.

I get out of the car, walk up the steps, and close the door behind me. I don't bother opening the shades before I kick off my shoes and dress. Stripping out of the one-piece lingerie, I toss it in the garbage. I walk to the bedroom naked, carrying the dress in my hand. I toss it into the laundry basket in my closet, then I grab some yoga pants and a sweatshirt. I walk to my bed and am about to climb in when I hear my phone ringing from the living room.

I walk out toward it, and I see it's Sandy.

"Hey," I say, walking back into my bedroom and getting under the covers.

"Hey," she says softly, "I was just calling to check in."

I breathe out. "I'm fine," I say, lying.

"Do you want me to come over for a girls' night?" she asks, and this is why I would do anything for her. She would drop anything and anyone for me.

"No," I say. "I'm going to watch television for a bit and then just chill out. Maybe take a nap, go to bed early."

"Okay," she says softly. "If you change your mind, you call me," she says, and I hum. "Promise?"

"I will," I tell her, and we both say bye. I toss my phone on the table by the bed and stare at the wall, then I flip the covers off me and get up and walk outside to the balcony. Sitting on the outside couch, I curl my feet under me and watch the water and the sky get darker and darker. I don't know how long I stay out here. Honestly, I don't even know if I fall asleep or not.

I get up and walk inside, closing the door and locking it. Then just to spite him, I unlock it. I walk to the kitchen and grab a water bottle, then go to my bed. I don't turn on any lights while I get ready for bed.

I turn the television on in my room and lie here flipping through the channels. I fall asleep in the middle of *Notting Hill* and wake up the next day stretching. My body hurts in certain places, and just like that, I think of him. His face, his smile, his smirk, his eyebrows pinched together. "He was an asshole to you," I say loudly, trying to argue with my heart. I huff and get out of bed, fixing the bed, and then get dressed for Sunday brunch at my parents'.

I grab a pair of black shorts and a blue jean shirt. I roll up the sleeves of the jean shirt and tuck the front in. I grab my black Chucks and a big black bag. I open the door and stop when I see a blue rose. I bend to pick it up and bring it to my nose.

A blue ribbon tied around it holds a note.

This was the color of your outfit on our first date.
I'm sorry.
T

I look around to see if I spot him, and even though I don't, I can't help but feel like I'm being watched. I walk back inside, looking at the garbage, but I can't do it, so instead, I put the flower in a single vase. I grab my sunglasses and walk outside, and the feeling is still here. But when I pull away from the curb to head to my parents', I still don't see him and figure it's all in my head.

Chapter Twelve

Hunter

I watch her walk down the step of her condo, her hair blowing back a bit, her sunglasses hiding her eyes. I sit across the street in an Audi, so she doesn't spot me.

I sat out here most of the night, too. I had Sandy call her and check on her since I knew she wouldn't answer my calls. That conversation was great. I was told in every single language known to mankind what an asshole I was. The only reason she called Laney was because, in the end, I was worried about her.

She didn't even call me back to tell me how she was; she just sent me a text with the finger emoji. I went home that night, the house stuffy and dark. I walked to the fridge, opening it and grabbing a water bottle. Not wasting a minute downstairs lounging, I made my way to the bedroom, which smelled just like her.

I laid down in the bed on the covers, grabbed the

pillow she slept on and smelled it, the words echoing in my mind, stupid and childish. I cringe just thinking about it, but dammit, she just ran out there. The minute I said the words, I knew I would regret them. I knew it was a mistake, but seeing her there, putting herself in danger was the push. What if Kelly had a gun? What if someone was watching? The what-ifs flew through my mind.

The thought of holding her in my hands with a bullet in her plays over and over in my mind, and I can't stop it. I didn't expect sleep to come to me, so it came as no surprise that I got up at five and made my way to her house with the blue rose I picked up yesterday in case she opened her door to me. I laid it on her doorstep with a note, then walked back to my car across the street. I watched it, and when she came out, my breath caught in my chest as my heart beat just for her. I followed her to her parents' house. When I watched her walk inside, I was about to get out and go ring the bell, but I thought of the scene it would cause.

Pulling away from the curb, I make my way over to my childhood home. Turning into the driveway, I'm not surprised to see my mother kneeling in front of the garden outside. She turns her head to see who pulled into her driveway and smiles when she sees me. She gets up from her knees when I get out of my car, taking off her gardening gloves. A smile fills her whole face. I look at her in her tight blue jeans and tank top; looking at her, you would think she was still in her thirties. A sun hat on her head covers her red hair. "There's my boy," she says, and her eyes are the same color as mine.

"Hey, Mom," I say, hugging her and breathing her in. She was a teen mom, getting pregnant with me at sixteen. My father took off as soon as she found out she was pregnant, and he never looked back. My grandparents weren't thrilled either, but they took it for what it was. She refused to drop out of school; she refused even take a year off. Instead, she homeschooled herself and graduated at the same time as her class with a one-year-old on her hip. Instead of going away, she went to community college part-time while working a full-time job. She defeated the odds and graduated with her CPA license. She bought the house the same day she opened her own office.

"I didn't know you were coming for a visit," she says, looking at me. "What's the matter?" she asks, taking the glasses off my face.

"I fucked up, Mom," I say, and she looks at me.

"Watch your mouth please," she says and then turns to walk into the house. I follow her, going straight to the kitchen and opening the fridge to grab a water bottle. She sits at the island and looks at me as I stand in the kitchen. "So, what did you do?"

"I met someone," I say, looking at her, and I see her smirk and then the twinkle in her eye. "Before you start, I don't even know if she is ever going to talk to me again."

"Oh, come on. It can't be that bad," she says, but as I tell her what happened, her mouth drops more and more. "Jesus, Hunter, how can you be so ... so ... so ..."

She gets up now, going to the fridge and grabbing the bottle of white wine to pour herself a glass. "So stupid."

I laugh at her and the way she says it. "I know, Mom. Trust me, I know."

"Okay, first," she says, grabbing the glass of wine, "the fact that you went on someone else's date is ridiculous."

I take a deep breath and exhale; for as long as I could remember, my mother made sure I had the deepest respect for women. When I'd started dating, she sat me down at the table and handed me a box of condoms; it was the most uncomfortable moment in my life. "Hunter," she had said, "just because you're horny doesn't mean you need to have sex with these girls." I'd thought or at least I'd hoped that the floor would open up and swallow me whole. "Don't take a girl's virginity just because you need to, you know. It's a special thing."

I got up from the table that night and left the condoms on the table, but during the next week, I'd found them in different places—my backpack, my side table, in my pencil case.

"I taught you better than that," she says, and I have no argument for her. None.

"I know, Mom," I tell her, and she goes to sit down now, looking at me.

"So," she says, and I look at her.

"So?" I say, leaning against the counter.

"What are you going to do about it?" She asks the loaded question.

"I have no idea," I say, crossing my arms over my

chest.

"Are you just going to give up?" She smirks at me.

"What do you want me to do, Mom?" I say. "She won't even answer her phone."

"There are other ways to get in touch with her," she starts. "Go to her house, knock on the door."

"Mom, she doesn't want to see me."

"I don't want to see you, yet here you are in my house," she says, and I roll my eyes at her.

"The only time you were ever mad at me was when I enlisted," I tell her, and she looks at me.

She slaps the counter in front of her. "I was not mad. I was scared of losing you. You little shit," she says, and I laugh, going to her and hugging her. Her arms wrap around my waist.

"I know, Mom," I tell her and kiss her head.

"Do you like this woman?" She looks up at me, and I nod. "I know that you would never intentionally hurt someone, so the big question is do you want her to forgive you because you want to be a good guy, or do you want her to forgive you because you want to see her again? Hold her hand again, smile at her again?"

"The second," I tell her honestly, and she smiles, and that look is back again.

"Well then, you need to put on your big boy panties."

"Boxers," I say.

She rolls her eyes. "Your big boy boxers and make her listen to you. I mean, you're a Navy SEAL. You save the world, so you can get a woman to talk to you," she says, and I smile. "Now, are you going to take your mother to lunch or what?" she asks me, and I just nod my head. "I have to change," she says and gets off the stool and jogs up the steps to get changed.

I take out my cell phone and send Laney a text.

Hey, wondering if you have a minute to talk.

I press send and see that it says delivered. Looking up the stairs, I watch my mother coming down. "Jesus, Mom," I tell her, taking in her pink linen loose shorts and spaghetti strap loose shirt. Her red hair is now down but braided at the side.

"What?" she says, looking down and not seeing anything wrong with her outfit.

"You have a lot of skin showing," I say with my hands pointing at her shoulders and then her legs with her white flip-flops.

"You think so?" She smiles at me. "Good. Hopefully, I can land me a date," she says, and I groan. "I'm a healthy forty-something woman," she starts and then grabs her big oversized purse, "with needs." And I put my hand to my head and stop in my tracks.

"I think I'm going to be sick," I say, putting my hand to my stomach right before we walk outside.

"Oh, stop it," she says. "I have to finish gardening when I get back," she says, taking in the garden she was weeding when I got here. "So where are you taking me?" she asks, getting in the car.

"Want Mexican?" I ask her, knowing full well she will never say no to Guadalupe's food.

"Yes," she says, grabbing her phone and snapping a picture of us together. "I'm going to put it on Instagram."

"You have Instagram?" I ask her since when, and she says, "The girls at work put me on that and Tinder."

I whip my head at her. "You are never ever allowed on Tinder. For fuck's sake, Mom, do you know the danger in going on Tinder?"

She looks at me, laughing. "Watch your mouth." She shakes her head while looking at her phone and typing something. "There is danger on there," she says with a smirk. "I saw Anthony on there."

"Oh my god." I close my eyes.

"Don't worry, I swiped left." She laughs. "But I did send him a dm telling him to change his picture."

"Can I have a normal mom conversation for once in my life?" I ask. "Like a conversation where I sound like the child and you sound like the adult?"

"What are you talking about now?" she asks, putting her phone down.

"Instagram, Tinder DM." I count on my fingers. "Moms shouldn't know that."

She rolls her eyes. "Oh, please," she says, and I don't even bother answering her or talking with her as I make my way over to Guadalupe's. She welcomes my mother with open arms, telling her she looks so good and sexy. She makes us all the food—literally all the food she has. And when I kiss my mother goodnight at the end of the night, she makes me promise to come back next Sunday with Laney. I make the promise, even knowing I might not be able to keep it.

Chapter Thirteen

Laney

Lunch at my parents' house slides by like a snail at a marathon race. My aunt Martha is there asking questions about Hunter. "So where is your man?"

"I don't have a man, Aunt Martha. He wasn't my man. He was a friend," I tell them as my mother eyes me from across the room.

"Leave her alone, Martha," my mother says, and then I just walk out of the room. Mom leaves me be until it's just the two of us. I am sitting in the backyard watching my father walk around the pool and scoop out the leaves when my mother walks out carrying a tray with a pitcher of sweet tea and three glasses on it.

She sits down in one of the chairs and pours me a glass. "So," she says, handing me a glass of tea with lemon in it. "What's the story?"

I look at my dad still by the pool. "He was just a

friend," I say, and my mother leans back.

"Oh, please," she says. "Just friends, my ass. You literally felt him up from head to toe last week," she points out.

"I was looking for his gun," I tell her honestly.

"Is that code for dick?" she asks, and I almost spit my tea out of my mouth. But I swallow it down, and then I choke on it, coughing.

"Mom!" I shout. "What are you saying?" I look at her, my eyes blinking.

"I'm asking if you were trying to ..." She moves her hands almost as if she's cupping something. "Trying to get to the package."

"What package?" my father asks when he approaches the table and sits down with us, my mother pouring him a glass of sweet tea.

"No package," I say, looking at my mother who sits back and just flips her wrist.

"So where is Hunter?" my father asks, leaning back in his chair. "Did he hurt you?" he asks. "I mean, I think I can take him if I had to." He looks at my mother who throws her head back and laughs. "I would have to do it at night, and I'd probably have to catch him off guard. But"—he points at me—"I could take him."

My mother leans forward in her chair and kisses his cheek. "Of course, you could, dear."

"He was just a friend."

"Was?" My father is fast to catch that.

"Is," I say. "Is a friend." I watch them watching me, and I know they aren't going to let it go. "Okay, fine. He called me stupid, childish, and impulsive."

I don't know why I expect them to take my side. I don't know why I expect my father to shoot his chair back and yell, but none of that happens. Instead, I get the stare down. "Why?"

"Pardon?" I say to them, looking first at my father and then my mother.

"Why?" my father starts. "Why did he call you that?"

"Why does that matter? The fact he said it is enough." I look at him.

"Honey," he starts, and I roll my eyes and groan, "he looks like a reasonable person."

"Okay," I say, throwing up my hands.

"So, a reasonable person isn't going to just come out and call people names. What happened before to make him go that route?"

"That route?" I say, my voice getting louder while my mother looks at me, trying to figure it out. "What does it matter what I did? What he said wasn't nice, and it wasn't true."

"I agree," my father says, "you are not stupid."

"I know," I agree and wait for him to continue.

"You can be childish, I mean, depending, and, honey, you are so impulsive."

"It wasn't my fault," I say, slamming my hands down on the table. "It was Sandy, okay? She was following her boyfriend, who, by the way"—I look at my mother—"is Anthony." Her mouth drops open. "Yeah." I nod. "Because she thought he was cheating on her."

My father shakes his head. "I knew this had to have

something to do with Sandy."

"It doesn't matter who or what it has to do with. He called me names, and I didn't like it."

"So, you left and didn't give him a chance to say sorry?" my mother says. "Honey, you know we have only your best interest at heart. But …"

"But nothing, Mom," I say softly. "What he said hurt me."

"Honey," my mother says, "he wouldn't get so upset if he didn't care."

"Doesn't matter," I say, shaking my head. "Doesn't matter." I turn to look at the pool, and no one says anything.

I kiss them both goodbye, and they make me promise to call them this week. Walking back into my house, I kick off my shoes and go outside. I walk to the railing and lean on it, watching the water. I feel eyes again on me. I scan the people on the beach, but it's late in the day and most people have packed up. I look around for his car, and it's not there. "It's all in your head," I tell myself, turning and going straight to bed.

I drag my ass the next morning, grabbing a pair of scrubs and not even making myself any coffee. I convince myself that my mood is just because I'm tired, but I'm lying. When I open the door to go to work, there is another rose; this time, a yellow one.

I look around, trying to see if he's here, but I don't see him. I bend to pick up the rose. Bringing it to my nose, I smell it before reading the note dangling from it.

The second day we spent together, the sun was

shining, but all I saw was your smile.

I'm sorry.

Hunter

I blink away the sudden itch to my eyes, then turn and walk back inside to place it in the vase with the blue one. I leave the notes hanging on them.

I look down the whole time I walk to the car, and then make my way to work. "Showtime," I say, grabbing my bag and walking into work. I smile at everyone and pretend nothing is wrong. Even when Teressa asks me about my weekend, I just say it was great.

After work, instead of driving home and sitting in my condo, I drive to the park. Getting out, I walk down the paved path that weaves around the green grass and huge trees. Strollers are everywhere because people are taking advantage of the good weather. I see a couple of people sitting together. A yoga class is on the right side, and a tai chi is on the other. I spot an empty wooden bench, so I sit on it and look around, watching the yoga class. When it's over, I see some of them stick around laughing. What the fuck is wrong with me? I knew him for one week—one—and it feels like I lost a piece of me, like it's missing.

The next five days are pretty much the same. After day three, I gave myself till Friday to snap out of it or I would kick my own ass. But it seems that every single time I think it's going to be okay, I open the door in the morning and sitting on the step is a rose with a different note. I just keep putting them together, telling myself it doesn't matter.

The last one was a black rose.

The color you wore when I fell for you.

I'm sorry.

Hunter

I'll leave you alone.

I don't know whether it's the fact he said he'd leave me alone or the fact that he said he fell for me, but I go back inside. Closing the door, I press my back to it, sliding down to the floor, and a sob rips through me as I hold the rose to my chest. Maybe this is what I need—to cry him out of my system.

I cry for five minutes, then get up and look in the mirror. Nothing will take away the bags that I have or the fact that my eyes are bloodshot and my nose red. I put on my sunglasses and make my way to work.

"Hey, are you okay?" Teressa asks when I walk out of my office.

"Yeah," I say, "I think I'm coming down with a cold."

"Well, you have the weekend to relax," she says, smiling. I go from patient to patient, the whole time my heart hurting, my mind empty.

I look at the next chart and see it's Anthony. I look up and walk into the examining room. "Hello there," I say, and then I spot Sandy sitting in the corner.

"Hey," she says, looking at me, and I try to avoid making eye contact with her. If anyone can see past my bullshit, it's Sandy.

"Let's see what we have," I say, looking at the X-rays. I work on his tooth, and when I finish, I smile at them both. "You should be good."

"Thank you so much," Anthony says. "I owe you."

"Don't worry about it," I tell him and then look at Sandy. "Call me later." I try to turn around, but the tone in her voice stops me.

"Oh, fuck no," she says, and I know with that tone we are having this out here. "You look like you lost a good ten pounds, and considering that you were skinny AF before, you look horrible."

"Wow," I say, "thanks." I fold my arms over my chest. Okay, maybe I lost a little weight but not ten pounds.

"I know what you need," she says, and I close my eyes, knowing this isn't going to be good. She is going to come up with a plan I'm not going to like, but I will go through with it to shut her up. Like the stakeout. "You need to get back out there. You had a taste of the D, and you need more of it." She then turns to Anthony. "Your friend Dante, call him. We are going on a double date. Tonight."

"Oh, no," I say, holding up my hands. "No fucking way."

"Anthony, call him," she says, and he takes out his phone and starts typing away. "Why aren't you calling him?"

"Because we're guys; we text," he tells her, then looks at me. "You know she is just going to hound you if you don't go along. Might as well give in now and suck it up for an hour."

"See," she says, pointing at him, "my man gets me."

"Whatever," I say, knowing she isn't going to let up. "I'll go for thirty minutes, then I have things to do."

"Like what? Starve yourself, watch Netflix?" she says, folding her arms over her chest.

"I don't even know why we are friends," I tell her and then turn to walk out when she starts laughing. Thirty minutes and she will get off my case. Thirty minutes sitting at a table on another blind date. *I can do this.*

Chapter Fourteen

Hunter

"Where the fuck is everybody?" I say, yelling from my office, and hear Rachel yelling back.

"Away from your cranky ass!" she yells, and I roll my eyes.

"There is a staff meeting at three!" I yell back.

"Oh, good, I can't wait!" she yells back, and I close my eyes. I've been in hell this week. I can't sleep, I can't eat, I can't do anything but see Laney's hurt face in my head going around and around on replay. I've tried calling her, but it goes straight to voice mail, so I know she blocked my number. The only thing I can do is leave her the notes, but even I can take the hint.

Every night, I go home exhausted, expecting to fall asleep. Hoping to fuck that sleep will come and take me. Instead, I toss and turn the whole night because the sheets still smell like her.

She was all around me. Monday morning, I placed the first rose on her doorstep. Then I went to my Audi and watched for her. She doesn't know this is my second car, so she didn't see me. I watched her pick the rose up and bring it to her nose; the need to hold her face in my hands almost had me running up the stairs. I expected her to text me. I expected something, but got nothing, so every night, I get her a rose and write my note, placing it outside her door.

Today, I placed the last rose on her doorsteps. Maybe she doesn't care. Maybe she's moved on. Maybe I felt more than she did.

I grab the file in my hand and walk downstairs, seeing everyone gathered for the staff meeting. Dante and Brian sit together and are going over the basketball game last night. Dominic is looking at something with Rachel, and Anthony sits alone while he types away on his phone, and I have the need to throat punch him.

If it wasn't for him and his dick, I wouldn't be in this predicament. "Okay, let's get this over with," I say, and everyone looks up. "I just got word that the VP is coming to town for a family vacation, so we have our work cut out for us. We handle the exterior; his team will handle the interior." I tell Rachel the address of the location, and she punches it in. The house pops up on the big projection screen.

Going over the plans, we look at the projection pictures as Rachel switches from angle to angle. When we think we have everything covered, Rachel laughs, and we all look over at her.

"Gentlemen," she says. Pressing the keys on her computer, she brings up the plans. "Here, here, and here," she says, pointing out three separate holes in our plan, so we take notes to tighten it up. Another reason I can't fire her.

"Good catch." I nod at her, and she just shrugs her shoulders. "So, if that is all," I say, concluding the meeting, "I think we are done. Have a great weekend because next week is going to be nuts." Rachel gets up, walking upstairs. I watch her, but I also notice Dante watching her. He waits for her to be out of earshot before turning to the guys. Something is up there, but I don't want to cross any lines. I'm putting the file back together when I hear Dante talk first, his voice lower than usual. "So, is this chick you're setting me up with really hot?"

I look at Anthony, who looks at me, and then looks at Dante right away. "Um ..."

"Is she really a dentist?" he says, and I slam my hand on the desk.

"You're setting Laney up with Dante?" I yell at him.

"No," he says, shaking his head. "Okay, fine. Maybe."

"You are not touching her." I point at Dante, then turn to Anthony. "You are not setting her fucking up."

"I'm not," he says, putting his hands up in surrender. "Sandy is."

"You're going on a blind date?" I hear Rachel say from behind him, and his face goes white. "Really."

He looks at the guys who are looking at him with a raised eyebrow.

I don't even bother waiting for whatever is going on there to play out. Instead, I turn to Anthony. "That woman," I say, closing my eyes and holding the bridge of my nose.

"She wouldn't take no for an answer," Anthony starts. "We went to fix my tooth, and well, Laney looked horrible, so Sandy got on her case." I look at Dante, who is looking at Rachel, who is glaring at him. If looks could kill, Dante would be roadkill.

"I can explain." Dante now gets up and looks at Rachel.

"This is so much better than I thought it would be," Dominic says, slapping Brian's arm. "We should have brought popcorn," he says, and Brian just smirks and shakes his head.

"I really don't need to hear your explanation on how you were going on a blind date tonight. Tonight," she says, walking to her desk and tossing her earpiece on it.

"Rach," he says, and now even I watch as he calls her that. No one calls her Rach. "He cornered me," Dante starts. "What was I supposed to do?"

"My sister cornered me," she starts, and Dante now glares back at Anthony.

"Your sister hates me," he points out.

"My mother cornered me, my aunt cornered me, my grandmother fucking cornered me," she shouts, "yet I went on zero blind dates!" She grabs her purse, looking at me. "I'm out."

"Where the fuck are you going?" Dante yells.

"None of your business," she snaps at him. "Enjoy

the date." She tries to walk past him, and he snatches her arm. Dominic and Brian now sit up. "Get your hands off me."

"Fuck this," he says, and his other hand comes out and grabs her face. "Enough," he says before he's kissing her. We are sitting here waiting to see if she wants this or not, ready to pick up the pieces of Dante's balls if she doesn't.

Standing up, Dominic digs in his pocket and pulls out a twenty, handing it to Brian. "Called it," Dominic says when Brian grabs the twenty and puts it in his front pocket of his jacket.

Dante lets go of Rachel and then grabs her hand, looking at us. "We're together."

"Really?" Anthony finally says. "Is that why you were sucking her face?"

Dante rolls his eyes at him but doesn't release Rachel. Anthony now looks at Dominic and Brian. "Any of you free for a blind date?" They both smirk, shaking their head. "She looks horrible," he says, looking at me, then back at the guys, hoping one of them bites. The guys avoid eye contact. "I feel bad."

"She doesn't look horrible," I tell him, and he turns his head at me questioningly.

"How would you know?" he asks.

"I …" I say, tapping my fingers on the desk, "I may follow her in the morning."

"Oh my god," Dante says and looks at the other two guys who just sit there with their eyes bulging out of their head.

"You follow her?" Anthony says, slapping his hand down on the table. "You follow her?" he repeats himself.

"I wouldn't have to follow her if it wasn't for you and your chafed dick!" I yell at him.

"Oh, no," he says, shaking his head. "You're not blaming me for this. You and that non-filter on your mouth got you in this mess. My dick was maybe ten percent responsible for it."

"If it wasn't for your dick, Sandy wouldn't have thought to follow you and then have Laney come also," I point out to him.

"MY DICK WAS RAW!" he yells. When I hear Rachel's laughter from beside me, I look at her to see her standing in front of Dante with his hands around her chest, pulling her close to him. Anthony stands now, but he's still talking. "Do you know how much sex one has to have for his dick to become raw?" When he looks around the room to see if anyone is going to answer him, he turns back. "A fuck ton." I roll my eyes. "I never thought it would be possible, but seven hours of sex will literally make your dick bleed."

"Did you take anything?" Dominic asks. "I think the most time I had sex was for three hours, but it was on and off."

"No." Anthony shakes his head. "My dick just saw her and boom, saluting." He uses his arm to point up.

"We are getting off topic here," I tell them.

Anthony turns to me. "Um, no, I think we are right on topic. You are a creepy stalker. And you need an intervention."

"I'm not a stalker, all right? I just wanted to make sure she was okay," I tell them and look up.

"Well, she's not," Anthony says. "She looks horrible." I glare at him. "Sandy said it; I didn't."

"Well, I'm coming to dinner with you tonight, so Dominic and Brian, you're out," I tell them. Dominic just puts his hands up, and Brian nods. Then I look at Anthony. "You're not coming either."

"Well, then how the hell do you plan on talking to her?" he asks, and I make a plan.

"You text Sandy and tell her we are going to Guadalupe's," I tell him.

"Amazing," he says, leaning back in his chair. "I've been dying for Mexican."

"You aren't coming," I tell him, and he raises an eyebrow. "You text Sandy and tell her to ask Laney to meet us there, but you don't come. I'll be there waiting for her."

"I don't know," Anthony says. "Sandy will be pissed."

"What is the worst that can happen? She doesn't give you sex, and your dick recuperates?" He shrugs his shoulders. "Now, text Sandy and make sure that Laney gets there at seven," I say, walking out of the room and putting a plan in motion. Anthony texts me that it's been done. I leave the office and go to Guadalupe and tell her my plans. She isn't happy with me when I tell her why I am in the doghouse, but she understands.

You see, Guadalupe and I met when we took a mission to Mexico to rescue a girl who was kidnapped, and she was in the same cell with the girl. What she didn't know was that her husband was one of the drug cartel's informants. She thought he was a cop, but when she found out he was dirty, she was going to go to the police, but he got to her before she had the chance.

Once we landed, she told the US government some key information about things, and they put her in the witness protection. No one really knows of the restaurant except the men who brought her here and some local surfers.

I grab a blanket and a wooden pallet, placing it on the beach. Surrounding it with lanterns, I grab a couple throw pillows and place them on either side of the pallet. Guadalupe comes out and starts putting some roses on the table and a lantern in the middle. "The food inside is all set up," she tells me at six thirty. "Good luck, Mr. Hunter," she says and walks away.

I sit on the blanket, taking off my shoes and socks. I shrug off my jacket and roll up the sleeves to my baby blue button-down shirt. I look at my watch every single second until I hear the crunch of the pebbles from her car. I take a deep breath in and exhale it. "This is it," I tell myself, my heart suddenly pounding faster than ever. My hands get sweaty and clammy, and I rub them on the front of my pants.

"Here it goes," I say to myself. I have no idea what the hell I'm going to tell her, and I'm suddenly kicking myself for not writing down a speech or something.

I get up and turn to look at the back of the restaurant. I see her shadow walking through the restaurant and looking around. I see her walk to the back of the restaurant and open the glass door. She doesn't see me until she walks to the edge of the deck. I watch her, and if she didn't knock me on my ass before, she does now.

She's wearing a tight black skirt with white stripes to her ankles paired with a long-sleeved turtleneck crop top, showing off just a little of her stomach. The same heels she wore to my house a week ago. Her hair is down and in curls, and I want nothing more than to bury my hands in it and kiss her. I raise my hand at her and smile just a bit.

She stands there for what seems like an eternity, but it's just a minute before she bends and takes off her heels. She steps out of them and walks down to the beach, looking at me from head to toe. She spots my bare feet and then looks to the side to see my shoes and socks are there.

"Hey," I say when she gets close enough.

"You're not Dante," she says, and I shake my head.

"No." I put my hands in my pockets because they itch to touch her. "I'm not Dante."

"What are you doing here?" she asks me, now standing next to the fake table that I set up for us on the beach right in front of me.

"Well, besides hijacking your date," I try to make a joke, "I wanted to see you."

"Really?" she says, folding her arms over her chest. "And why is that?"

"I want to apologize and tell you I'm sorry to your face," I tell her. I'm so nervous now that maybe she really doesn't care.

"And you couldn't do this yesterday, or maybe the day before that?"

"I didn't know how," I tell her the truth.

"You left all those roses, all those notes. Not once thinking to knock on my door, yet now you know?"

I take a deep breath. "Today was the last rose I was going to leave you," I tell her, and I see something flash in her eyes. "Everyday, I would leave the rose and wait in the car, hoping to get the courage to run out and talk to you, but I couldn't." This time, I step closer to her, hoping she doesn't push me away. "I couldn't, or I wouldn't because I didn't want to hear you say that you didn't want to see me again. I didn't want to think about not being able to see you again." I stand in front of her now. "I'm so sorry I called you stupid and reckless," I say, and she looks down and brushes away a tear that started to roll down her face. I put my hand under her chin, lifting her face to look at me. "I'm so, so sorry."

"I'm not reckless," she says, and I just watch her. I memorize her face, so I make sure I never forget it. "I will admit it wasn't my finest moment, and I shouldn't have let Sandy go off like that. But—"

I cut her off. "I don't know what I would do if something happened to you because of being at the wrong place at the wrong time," I tell her, and she just looks at me. "The first girl we had to rescue was in Panama with her best friend who decided she wanted to have a fun, carefree night. Well, she was the one who was taken and beaten and raped over and over again for three straight days. When we finally rescued her, she was barely holding on."

"Oh my god," she says and comes closer to me, reaching out to touch my face. "Hunter."

"I know it's not the same thing," I tell her. "I know that Sandy would never do that." My hand drops from her face, settling on her hip. "I just … I saw red. So much could have happened. Seeing you there, seeing Sandy jumping and bouncing, if Kelly had a gun and shot her or you by accident." I shake my head. "I can't."

She gets on her tippy toes, leaning in to me. "I missed you," she says softly, the waves crashing in the background, almost drowning her out.

"I watched you from Saturday till Sunday night," I tell her. "I even went to your parents' house with you." She gasps. "I know it's creepy, but I had to see if you were okay."

"No one has ever cared enough to do that," she says. "I broke up with Trevor, and he didn't even do so much as send a text. He sent a delivery person with my stuff the next day."

"He's a dick," I say to her, my arms wrapping around her waist to bring her closer to me. "Will you forgive me?" I ask her and hold my breath.

Her hands go to the collar of my shirt. "You took off your shoes and socks," she says, smiling and looking down. "You did that for me."

"I won't tell you how much it's killing me." I laugh. "But, yeah."

"Will you take me home?" she asks me. "To your

house?" I look at her. "For the weekend."

"For the month, if you want," I tell her, leaning in to her and bending my head. "For the year, for as long as you will stay," I say right before I kiss her lips, my heart finally, finally beating normal.

Chapter Fifteen

Laney

The minute I saw him, my heart literally skipped a beat, jumped up, and did cartwheels. You name it—it did it. I took off my shoes and walked to him on the beach.

He stood there next to what looked like a beach picnic. Pillows all around the wooden crate. Hearing the things he tells me, hearing him tell me his fears made everything clear.

"Will you take me home?" I ask him. "To your house?" He looks at me, his eyes shining. "For the weekend."

"For the month, if you want," he tells me right away, bending his head down to me and resting his forehead on mine. "For the year, for as long as you will stay," he whispers to me right before he kisses my lips. My hands wrap around his neck, my body finally relaxing against him.

"This whole thing could have been avoided if you had just come to my door and talked to me," I tell him.

"What if you turned me down?" he says, the fear in his eyes.

"What if I didn't, and we avoided this? Yes, I was mad, and, yes, I might have exaggerated a bit, but what you said hurt me," I tell him.

"I'm sorry," he whispers. "Forgive me and come home with me."

"Can we eat first?" I tell him when I let go of him. "I kind of haven't been hungry lately but all of a sudden." I don't say anything else because he kisses my neck and runs back to the restaurant.

"Sit. I'm getting all the food," he says over his shoulder. I sit on the sheet with my feet on the side of me. I watch the water and then hear the door close. Turning, I see him coming out with two trays. "I think I got it all," he says, and I get up to help him. I grab a tray, and the smell of the spices hits me right away.

"She made fresh tamales this morning, and she tried a new recipe, she said, for the burrito bowl. She wants you to tell her if it's good," he says, and I place my tray down on the makeshift wooden table. Hunter kneels, placing his tray on the table, and when I see tacos and enchiladas, my mouth waters.

"I want all the food," I say to him when he sits next to me, and he leans over and kisses me. He hands me a plate, and I fill it with more food than I can possibly eat, but I'm going to give it my best shot.

We eat while he fills me in on how miserable he

was the whole week. I look at him. "I wasn't that much better," I tell him about how excited I was to see the roses, yet all I really wanted was for him to come and talk to me.

I finish eating and lean back on the pillows. "I think I'm going to burst," I say, and he gets up, stacking the plates on the trays. "What's the rush?"

He looks at me. "I haven't had you for seven days; that's the rush." He just piles everything and then gets up. "Grab your shit."

I laugh at him. "Seven days isn't that long," I point out to him.

"It's almost as if it's a year," he says, and I get up and help him carry in the dishes. It takes us three trips, but we finally have everything cleaned up. "Okay," he says while I put on my shoes, "where are your car keys?"

"In my purse," I tell him. "Why?"

"I'm going to drive," he tells me, reaching his hand out.

"Where is your car?" I ask him, handing him the keys.

"Anthony dropped me off," he says, smiling when he takes my my hand and brings my fingers to his mouth where he kisses me.

"I was hoping you would forgive me."

"You did this to yourself," I tell him. "Next time, suck it up and come see me."

"There isn't going to be a next time," he tells me, opening the door for me and kissing me before I get in. He has to put the seat all the way back when he gets in, and I laugh at him.

"It's fucking tight," he says, starting the car and making his way to his house. When we pull up, I see the white Audi that was parked in front of my house the whole week.

"That's your car?" I say, pointing at it, and he nods.

"Yeah, it's my undercover car," he says, getting out and smashing his knee on the steering wheel. "Motherfucker," he says, and I laugh, getting out of the car and meeting him.

"Are you okay?" I ask him as he scowls at me. "Don't worry, I'll kiss it better." I wink at him as he takes my hand and pulls me to his front door.

"Do you want to go outside or …?" he says, unlocking the door. I don't answer him. Instead, I walk in, wait for him to follow, and then grab his hand. I dump my purse on the floor and head straight for the stairs. I walk up the stairs toward his bedroom.

I walk into his room, the dim light glowing behind his headboard. The sheets are a mess, looking almost like they have been tangled. "What happened?" I ask, walking to his bed and seeing the cover twisted in a ball, the sheet pulled out and flipped over.

"I," he starts saying, and I look at him and see that all the pillows are on top of each other. "I had a hard time sleeping, and I just wanted to smell you."

"Oh, my," I whisper and pick up a pillow and bring it to my nose. "This is mine."

"I know," he says, coming to me. "I would sleep with it in my arms."

I put the pillow down and go to him, my hand going to his face. He turns his face to kiss my palm, his hand going to my hip. "I missed you." I tell him the truth. "So, so much," I tell him and lean up, kissing his lips, his mouth opening for me, and my tongue meeting his. Both of us moan into each other's mouth. His hands go from my hips to my tits. He cups them, and my nipples pebble under his touch. He pushes my shirt up, taking the bra with his fingers and rolling my nipples as he does.

My hands go to his hips. I move my index finger inside his waistband from his hips to the front of his pants, brushing my finger against the tip of his cock. I know right away it gets to him because he pinches my nipples even harder, and the feeling hits me straight in my core.

I can't wait anymore, so I push away from him and unsnap his belt. The sound of me pulling down his zipper echoes in the room. Pushing his pants down around his hips, I drop to my knees and look up at him right before I lick the pre-cum off his cock, his eyes watching me as I take his head in my mouth.

I watch his eyes close when I take him deeper and deeper into my mouth. "Fuck," he hisses, grabbing my hair. I take him into my mouth again and again and again. His eyes open, and he looks down at me while he slowly fucks my face. My hand grips him at the base, and I work him as he gets bigger and bigger in my mouth. "Fuck, I'm going to come," he says. He tries to take his cock out of my mouth, but I stop him and just take him deeper until he throws his head back and comes down my throat. "Laney." I swallow all of him, letting him go when I know he's done. "That was …" he says, his chest heaving. "That was …"

"Good?" I laugh at him, trying to help him fill in the blank.

"Better than good," he says, untucking the rest of his shirt and then slowly unbuttoning it. "But you know what's better?" The look he gives me makes my stomach have all the butterflies in the world. "Reciprocation," he says, tossing his shirt on the floor and kicking off his shoes.

Once he's naked, he walks over to me. Grabbing my shirt, he pulls it and my bra over my head. "Hmm," he says, leaning in and taking a nipple into his mouth, then going to the next one and humming as well. He bites it just a touch, and my back arches. His hands go to my hips, and he peels off my skirt, leaving me in a little, and I mean little lace thong. He runs one finger over the front; goose bumps fill my whole body, and then he grabs the sides and rips them away from my body. I look at him shocked, and all he can do is smirk at me. "Oops, my bad," he says right before he pushes me on the bed and buries his face between my legs.

Chapter Sixteen

Hunter

Something tickles my nose, making me slowly open my eyes. I look down and see that Laney's hair is half on my face. She moves like a ninja when she sleeps. I move the hair from my face and look over.

After I made her come on my tongue, I made her come on my finger and then my cock. Then we took advantage of the tub, her bent over the side, soap suds everywhere … just thinking about it makes my cock rise. "Not a chance in hell." I hear grumbled from beside me.

"What?" I ask, looking down at her. When we got out of the bath, she made us fix the bed. I didn't get it since we were going to sleep in it, but I would have gone outside and hung the fucking moon if she asked.

"I feel a baseball bat on my leg," she says, and I laugh because I'm on my back and her leg is thrown over my hips and so is her hand.

I roll to my side, grabbing her in my arms. Her leg is still over my hip, but her pussy is right where it needs to be. It's open and waiting, but it's not me who does anything. She's the one who slowly tips her hips. I hum when she does it again. "I'm on the pill," she says, "and after Trevor, I have gotten tested every six months since."

"I'm clean," I tell her. "We get blood tests every six months." I don't tell her anything else when she slides right down on me. We both groan when I'm finally buried all the way in her. We don't say anything to each other while our hips rock slowly in sync, and when she comes, she buries her face in my neck, and I follow her.

"I can get used to waking up like that every single day," I say to her as she snuggles into me, my cock still buried in her.

"What do you want to do today?" she asks me.

"Um, I'm pretty much happy doing exactly this today," I say to her, and she tilts her head back, laughing. I lean forward and kiss her lips.

"I need food, and you need food," she says, "so how about you get the coffee ready, and I'll clean up?"

I nod at her, and she rolls away from, getting up out of bed and walking to the bathroom. I get up and follow her into the bathroom, finding her in the shower with her hair tied on top of her head. She spots me coming in. "Oh, no, you don't." She laughs when I open the door.

"There is enough room in here for two," I tell her.

"There is enough room in here for a football team," she says.

I stay on my side, getting out of the shower first.

"Do you have some shorts and a T-shirt I can borrow?" she says. Getting out of the shower, she wraps a big white towel around her while I'm slipping on a pair of boxers and shorts.

"I like you like that," I tell her, winking at her. "Actually," I say, grabbing her a pair of shorts, "I like you without the towel."

"Yeah, well, I don't think me sitting buck ass naked outside will go well with your neighbors."

I walk over to her with a pair of shorts in my hands, extending them to her. "No one gets to see you naked but me," I say, kissing her lips. "You need to bring over clothes." I turn to grab a T-shirt. "I'll make room today, and we can run over to your house and grab some things."

"Or," she says, "I can just borrow from you till the next time."

"Nah," I say, shaking my head, "I like my plan better."

I kiss her neck and walk out of the room to go downstairs and open the back windows. I start the coffee, doing mine first and then hers. By the time I finish her coffee, I see her coming downstairs, wearing my shorts rolled at the waist a couple of times, the black T-shirt tied in a knot on the side, and her hair still tied up.

"Is that mine?" she says, pointing at the full cup of coffee.

"Yeah," I say and lean down to kiss her, and then I hear the front lock open. I turn my head, knowing only three people have my code—Anthony, Rachel, and my mother.

Laney looks over my shoulder, and my guess is correct when I see my mother walk in. Except she doesn't really dress like a mom. She's wearing green shorts rolled up, making them even shorter, and a black silk button-down shirt with her sleeves rolled up. A chunky necklace hangs around her neck, and she is wearing a chunky watch with two bracelets, and beige and black strappy heels make the whole outfit. Laney gasps next to me. "Oh my god."

"Oh my gosh," my mother says with a smile. "Isn't this a nice surprise?" She closes the door, putting her purse on the table. Walking in, she clinks her heels on the floor, her long red hair flowing.

She comes over, smiling. "Mom," I say, then look at Laney who opens her eyes even more. My mother comes to me and kisses my cheek. "You didn't even call."

She ignores me like only my mother can. "Laney, it's so nice to finally meet you." She walks around me, grabbing Laney by the shoulders and kissing her cheeks. "I'm Joanna."

Laney still looks in shock. "Um, hello," she says.

"She is absolutely stunning," my mother continues.

"Mom, she's right here," I tell her, and my mother laughs.

"I didn't say anything wrong," she says. "Did you guys eat yet?" She looks at us, then walks to the counter and sits on one of the stools. "Looks like you just got up."

"Yeah," I say, leaning against the counter. I look over at Laney who has her arms wrapped around her waist. I lean over, hugging her shoulders and bringing her close to me, then kissing the side of her head. She looks up at me and smiles, wrapping her arms around my waist.

My mother smiles at us and claps her hands. "We should go out for brunch," she says, and I look down at Laney.

"Want to go out for brunch?" I ask her.

"Sure, that sounds great." She smiles at me and then my mother. "I'm going to go get dressed," she says, walking away from me and almost running up the stairs.

"She is gorgeous," my mother says. "Good thing you got your head out of your ass."

I shake my head at her, kissing her cheek again, then I walk up the stairs to the bedroom. Walking into the room, I see Laney walking around the room. "Hey," I say, and she turns to me.

She holds up her hand with the black scrap of lace I ripped off her. "How the hell am I supposed to go to brunch with your mother when I have no panties?" she says, and she doesn't give me a chance to answer because she paces around the room, picking up her clothes. "This is almost as bad as doing the walk of shame the next morning."

"Laney," I say, smiling at her that she's nervous, but she doesn't look at me while she pulls my T-shirt off and stands in front of me shirtless. I look at her and lick my lips.

"Are you out of your mind?" she says. I look at her confused. "You can't even think of touching me with your mother downstairs. Your mother who doesn't look like a mother, by the way. She looks like a goddamn runway model." She continues talking, clipping on her bra and turning it to pull it up over her arms. "I thought she was an ex."

"I've never brought anyone here," I tell her. "I've actually never had a relationship."

She stops moving. "What do you mean? Like you never had a girlfriend?"

"Don't get me wrong," I say, going to her. "I've dated, just not exclusively." I grab her hips. "Now don't freak out. Get dressed, and let's go have brunch with my mother."

"What if she doesn't like me?" she whispers. "What if she thinks I'm a hussy?"

I throw my head back and laugh. "You are not a hussy."

"I'm wearing your clothes the day after." She puts her arms around my waist. "That screams hussy."

"Get dressed, Laney," I tell her, and she just nods at me. "After brunch, we'll go to your house and grab some stuff."

"Okay," she says and walks to her skirt, picking it up and slipping it on. I walk to my closet and grab a pair of light blue jeans ripped at the knees and a light blue button-down shirt. I leave the first three buttons open and roll up the sleeves, putting on my brown belt and grabbing my white running shoes. I walk out and see Laney sitting on the bed bending over and tying her shoes.

She shakes her head. "I see now where you get your style from."

"I got it from my mom." I joke with her, going to the bathroom and fixing my hair.

Laney sticks her head in the bathroom. "I'm ready," she says.

I look over at her, and she is dressed exactly as she was last night with her hair in long waves. I walk to her, kissing her, and then grab her hand. "Let's go."

I walk down the stairs and find my mother outside sitting in one of the lounge chairs. "Mom!" I yell from the kitchen.

She swings her legs off the lounger and walks to us. "How old is she?" Laney whispers to me.

"In her forties," I say. "She was a teen mom." I smile.

"I think she looks younger than I am." She smiles.

I roll my eyes. "I can't tell you how many times I got asked if she was my sister."

"Laney, you look wonderful," she says, coming in. "I love that skirt."

"Thank you," she says, looking down.

"I'll drive," I say, grabbing the keys to my car. "Where should we go?"

"Oh, let's go to the Ivy. They make amazing mimosas," my mother says when she grabs her purse and puts on her aviator glasses.

"Oh, I can go for a mimosa," Laney says, "or a martini." I look at her, and she winks at me.

"We can do both," my mother says, walking in front of us. "I don't even have a date tonight," she says, and Laney tries to hide her laugh when I groan. "He gets cranky when I mention dating and sex."

"Mom, seriously," I say out loud, opening the door for Laney and then for my mother. "Can we tone it down?"

"Nope," she says, getting in the back and smiling. "Not even a bit."

Laney gets on her tippy toes and laughs, kissing me. "This is going to be fun after all."

I close both doors, then walk around the car and get in. I make my way to the Ivy, and I remember pulling up two weeks ago in a whole different frame of mind. When I pull up to the valet, Laney turns to my mother. "We had our first date here."

"Really?" my mother says. "How fun."

"Well, it was fun till he put a damper on the party by telling me the dangers of drinking by myself," Laney mentions.

"He's such a buzzkill, my kid," she says, laughing when the valet opens the door for Laney and then my mother. "Thank you," my mother says, getting out of the car and walking to the hostess stand while Laney waits for me.

"Three for the garden." I hear my mother say, and then she turns to me. "Out in the garden is okay, right?"

"Yeah, that's fine," Laney says, and I just follow the women as they chat on the way to the table. My mother takes a seat first, and Laney sits in the chair in front of her, so I sit in the middle of them.

"It's such a beautiful place, isn't it?" she asks Laney, mostly while I look around, scanning the restaurant. A couple of men at the bar have turned around, but half the tables inside are empty since the weather is so nice. Most of the tables outside are full.

My mother picks up a menu and is reading it when the waiter comes to the table to give us the specials. My mother orders a bottle of champagne and a pitcher of freshly squeezed orange juice.

"Mom, a whole bottle?"

"Oh, here he goes," Laney says, looking at her menu.

"Honey," she says, looking at me, "you're the badass ex-Navy SEAL guy with a security firm. If we aren't safe, we have other issues."

I groan out loud when Laney agrees with her, nodding her head. The waiter comes over with a silver bucket and places it between my mother and me. "Here you go," he says, showing her the bottle of champagne. She just nods her head and smiles. He peels off the foil wrapper, then unwinds the twist tie holding in the cork. He slowly turns the cork, and after it pops with a soft pop, he pours each of our champagne glass halfway. Putting the bottle of champagne in the silver bucket, he moves it to the side, and another waiter comes with a pitcher of orange juice to fill the glass to the top.

"Thank you," Laney and my mother both say at the same time.

"Shall we toast?" my mother says, grabbing her glass. Laney grabs hers. "To love."

Laney looks down and then up again at me. "To love." They clink their glasses and look at me.

"I'm not drinking when I have to watch you two," I say, and Laney throws her head back and laughs. "What? It's true."

"He definitely doesn't get that from me," my mother says, and I hear my name being called. I look over and see Dominic walking to us.

"I thought that was you," Dominic says, walking to me, his black hair falling onto his forehead. His aviator glasses hiding his blue eyes. His jeans tight with a white T-shirt.

"Hey, are you here by yourself?" I ask him, standing to shake his hand, and he nods his head.

"You have to join us," I say and then look at Laney. "Laney, this is Dominic. He works for me." Laney stands halfway from her chair and puts out her hand to shake his. "And this is my mother," I start to say, and then I'm shocked when Dominic talks.

"Joanna," he says, looking at her. My mother smiles, getting up and turning and looking at him.

"Dominic, it's so nice to see you again," she says, grabbing his arms and kissing his cheek.

"You know each other?" I ask, and Dominic doesn't answer, but my mother does.

"Yeah." She turns to sit down. "We date occasionally."

I look at Dominic, who opens his mouth to say something, but nothing comes out. "I mean, dating is a stretch." She smiles and takes a drink from her mimosa.

"I had no idea," Dominic says, and I just glare at him.

"This is going to be fun," Laney says, grabbing her own mimosa and draining it. "Can I have another?"

"Sure," my mother says, not even caring that I'm still standing and having a face-off with Dominic.

"I can explain," he starts, and I just shake my head. The questions are running through my head.

"Sit," I tell him, and he walks over to the empty seat, which faces me.

"Explain," I tell him, and Laney bites her lip.

"Absolutely not," my mother says. "What Dominic and I do is not up for discussion. And frankly," she says, filling her glass even more, "if I have to explain what we do, we have other issues." I groan, Laney and my mother laugh, and Dominic looks like he wants to die. "Besides, what we do in our private time is private." She looks at Dominic. "Isn't that right, Dom?"

"He hates that nickname," I tell her, and he just shrugs.

"This isn't happening. How the hell did you two meet?"

Dominic starts to talk, and my mother talks over him. "Tinder."

I look at them. He turns his head to look at my mother who looks back at him, almost like she is daring him to say something otherwise. He doesn't do any of this. Instead, he pushes his chair back so hard it screeches. Standing up, he says, "Let's go." He puts his hand out to my mother, and I expect her to kick him in the balls, but she pushes her chair back, then reaches out and takes his hand. She takes his hand in a way that shows me that it isn't the first time. "Enough of this shit," he says to her. "No more games, baby. No more pushing me away pretending." She smiles at him as he pulls her away.

"I'll call you tomorrow," she says over her shoulder.

"I think I'm going to be sick," I say to Laney, who looks at me and laughs.

"Your friend is dating your mother," she points out. "Oh my god, this must be killing you."

"Oh, I'm going to be killing someone. You can bet on that," I say, picking up my mimosa and downing it.

Epilogue One

Hunter

Seven months later . . .

I pick up my spoon and click the wine glass in front of me, the chattering of the people around us stopping when I stand. I look around the reception area and spot all the hard work we did over the past couple of days. Two days of hustling the tables and chairs all over the place. We moved it from one place to the other until the bride was happy, and it took about fifty tries. Okay, fine, three but when you're moving all the tables, it feels like fifty.

Ten round tables line up in three rows around a makeshift wooden dance floor. The white linen tablecloths cover the plastic white tables. White floral centerpieces are the only thing on the tables now with candles all around it.

Ten wooden poles planted into the ground hold up string lights zigzagging all the way around to give us some light on the beach. If I thought moving the tables was something, I then see the lights and think of what a bitch it was to hang those up. The ladder doesn't really work in the uneven sand, trying to hammer in the nails so we can hang them. Then having one of the girls walk by and say you should have hammered before planting them in the sand. All five men out there just glared at them as they shrugged and walked away. None of us actually admitted we should have done just that. Instead, we bitched, moaned, and swore the whole fucking time.

But I just smile and look over at the bride, trying my best not to piss her off. "So, it's time for the best man's speech," I say.

I look over at Anthony who is sitting next to his wife, his arm around her shoulder, her back to his chest, while one hand holds her pregnant stomach.

"Thank you all for coming to celebrate Anthony and Sandy," I start, and the whole crowd cheers. I smile, looking at everyone when I feel a hand hold my leg and look down at Laney. She sits there in her rose gold dress with her hair tied at the base of her neck, smiling up at me. "These two ... I don't even think Tinder knew what to do with them," I say, looking over at them, "except to match them."

Everyone laughs, especially Anthony and Sandy, who throws her head back. "I never thought I would see him settle down, never thought he would find the one, but he did." I smile and look down at Laney.

"Sandy, he's a lucky guy," I tell her, and I look at Anthony who just nods, "to have found someone who is exactly, and I mean, exactly, like him." A couple of people pick up their wine glasses and cheer. "I know he is going to be the best husband and the best father, and if he isn't …" I look down and then up at Sandy. "I'm sure you will point him in the right direction," I say. "To the newlyweds." I hold up my glass. "May your love never die."

I take a sip and sit back down next to Laney. "I fucking hate speeches," I tell her. "Hate them."

"You did really well," she says, leaning over, and I kiss her. "So, well, I might have a surprise in store for you when we get home." She raises her eyebrows.

I wink at her, my heart filling when she says the word home. Home. Our home. It took me a whole two weeks to ask her to move in with me; it took two whole weeks of silently sneaking her shit out of her house and putting it in mine. We would stop by her house, and she would pack a little bag, but unbeknownst to her, I was also filling a bag on the side. Until she finally had nothing left in her condo. It wasn't as if I had to twist her arm; she was practically there all the time. Every night, we ate dinner together, talking about our day while sitting outside watching the stars before going to bed together. And when she wasn't, well, I would go to wherever she was and make sure she came to me.

I hear the song "Meant to Be" come on, and I stand. "Will you dance with me?" I say, holding out my hand to her. She nods, turning in the chair and standing up.

She puts her hand in mine, and we walk to the makeshift dance floor, no one following us. Instead, everyone seems to be interested in their own conversations. Anthony and Sandy visit each table, thanking their guests for coming. A couple of people standing at the improvised bar are doing shots.

I put my hands around her waist as she puts one hand around my neck and one on my chest right in the middle over my heart. I wonder if she feels its erratic beat. "I like this song," I tell her, and she just looks up at me, her eyes sparkling, wrapping both hands around my neck. My hands getting clammy, I twine my fingers around the back of her waist.

"It's catchy," she says, and I start, my heartbeat echoing in my ears.

"If you listen to the words, it's kind of our theme song," I tell her while we go in a small circle. Everyone watches us, pretending that they aren't. Laney doesn't notice anything as she looks at me.

"Really?" she says, and she cocks her head, listening to the words. She doesn't notice that I've stopped dancing and am now standing in front of her. She looks at me now, and then I do what I have been dying to do since she first threw sass at me.

When I get down on one knee, her hands fly to her mouth as she looks at me. "I have no idea what the future holds, and I have no idea how the path will be." I smile and swallow, my mouth so dry. "I have no idea if it's going to be rocky or if it's going to be smooth sailing, but I am sure of one thing, and that is that I want you by my side through it all," I say, and she cries and laughs. "I want you to be there holding my hand, yelling at me for not listening, and rolling your eyes at me—my all-time favorite," I say, reaching into my suit pocket and taking out the engagement ring I bought when she moved in. "What do you say, Laney? Do you want to ride with me?"

She stares at me, not saying anything, until Sandy yells, "Will you answer him so we can get on with my wedding?" She turns to look at her best friend who stands now by the dance floor with all our friends. My mother stands there hugging Corina as they both cry. Gary stands there proudly; he was the only other person who knew. I went traditionally with asking for her hand in marriage. Sandy was the one who said I had to do it today.

"Yes," she says with tears running down her face. "Yes, I'll marry you." She reaches down, taking my face in her hands and kissing me. "You are so romantic." She laughs, and I finally slip the two-carat round diamond ring on her finger, taking her in my arms and turning her around.

Epilogue Two

Laney

Three years later . . .

"I can't believe we are actually selling this house," I say, looking over at Hunter standing in the middle of the empty kitchen. I'm standing outside on the deck, looking at the ocean.

"Babe," he says, "we outgrew this house two years ago." He steps outside and puts his hands on my ever-growing stomach, our daughter kicking his hands the minute he touches me.

"She's awake." He smiles at me, and I take in his face, the little wrinkles that are around his eyes, creasing every single time he smiles. "Hello, princess," he says, leaning down to talk to my stomach. She already has him wrapped around her little finger, and she's not even born. "I can't wait to meet you," he says, and I run my hands through his hair.

Three years ago, when he proposed to me, and I said yes, I thought we would be engaged for a while before getting married. I was wrong. The next day, my mother and Joanna showed up with seven bride books. *Seven.* They walked in and had everything planned, no surprise there. They had a plan in place and had a wedding date set for three months later. I laughed at them, thinking there was no way we could plan a wedding in that time.

Joanna looked at me with a smile, almost like a smirk, and I knew I was in trouble. She sat at my table outside and asked questions.

"How big of a wedding do you want?" she asked, leaning back in her chair.

"I'm not sure," I answered honestly.

"Well, do you want four hundred people?" my mother asked. "Or do you want intimate?"

"Definitely intimate," I said the truth and looked up to see Hunter shake his head, almost saying I was setting myself up. My mother took notes.

"Do you want an indoor wedding or an outdoor wedding?" Joanna then asked. I looked over at my mother for her to help me, but all she did was tap her pen on the pad.

"Um," I said, "Hunter?" I turned to look at him. "What do you think?"

"I don't give a shit as long as I get to marry you," he said, and I glared at him and made a mental note to hurt him really bad when his mother wasn't around.

"If I had to pick, I would love to get married on

the beach at sunset but have the reception in the air conditioning."

"Yes," Joanna said. "No one needs to sweat in a nice dress."

"What about the hotel on the beach with the restaurant with the panoramic views?" my mother asked. "What's it called?"

"Seven seven seven," Joanna said. "I know the owners. I do their books, so I'll make a call. They owe me a favor."

"Oh, perfect," my mother said and made more notes.

"Stop taking notes," I told her, and she just looked up at me.

"It's my job to take notes," she said to me, and I had no idea what the hell she was talking about. "During this conversation, my job is to take notes, and Joanna's is to ask the questions."

"Why?" I asked.

"Because your mother seems to think you won't tell me to fuck off since I'm Hunter's mother," Joanna said, laughing, then leaned over to put her hand on mine. "I told them that it was only a matter of time." She winked at me, and I had to say she was the most down-to-earth person I had ever met. Sometimes, I forgot she was Hunter's mother and not just another one of my friends.

"Now the big question," my mother said. "Dress."

"I'm not wearing an ugly mother of the groom dress," Joanna said right away, "and I'm not making your mother wear anything drabby either." She looked at my mother who nodded. "We are young, independent

women who raised two amazing kids. We should not have to wear long sleeves and low heels."

"Yes," my mother agreed. "No ugly brown for me. I want fuchsia."

"That's a great color with your hair," Joanna said, then looked at me. "I know the wedding designer from that TLC show Say Yes to the Dress*," Joanna said.*

"Pnina?" my mother asked, and Joanna nodded.

"Yes, I do her American taxes," she said.

"Oh my god," my mother said, "you think she would design the dress?"

"I don't see why not. I can call and ask her. Why don't we get our dresses designed also?" Joanna asked.

That was the way the whole night went, and by the next week, everything was booked. I got my ceremony on the beach, and the restaurant was shut down that night just for us. Joanna said it was comped. I didn't believe her, but Hunter just said to let it be.

Two weeks later, we were in New York and I had the dress of my dreams designed.

I knew right away it was the dress when I walked down the aisle two and a half months later and Hunter had tears coming down his face. It was perfect, our wedding was perfect, and so was the fact I was hiding the secret that I was carrying his child. A surprise I told him that night when he peeled me out of my wedding dress. There in the middle of my stomach was a removable tattoo of a bow.

"What is this?" he asked with a smile, sitting on the bed as I stood between his legs in my garter and bra.

"It's your groom's gift," I told him, and he looked up at me. "We're having a baby," I whispered the words before I saw him cry for the second time that night.

Eight months later, I gave birth to our son, who came out with a full head of black hair and eyes exactly like his father.

"Mommy, Mommy, Mommy." I hear Logan while he runs into the house we brought him home to. I turn to watch him, his hair flying everywhere as he jumps into his father's arms.

"I had ice cream," he says, and I don't have to ask him what kind because he has chocolate on his nose.

"Where is Grandma?" I ask him and look over their shoulder to see Joanna walk in, or actually waddle a bit. Yup, my mother-in-law, grandmother to almost two, is six months along with twins.

"Don't blame me," she says, and I look at her. Even pregnant, she rocks it; there are no maternity clothes for her. Nope, she refused. So, she stands there in a long skirt flowing around her with a tight tank top. "It's them." She points at her stomach. "You can blame them. All I did this week was eat ice cream. Tubs and tubs of it. I'm surprised my ass fit through the door," she says, going to Hunter and kissing his face. "Hey, honey."

"Where is Dominic?" Hunter asks.

"How many times have I asked you to call me dad?" Dominic says, walking in with a smile while Hunter groans.

"Is Uncle Dom your dad?" Logan asks, and Hunter shakes his head while we all laugh.

"Did you tell Mom and Dad that we went shopping for your new room?" Joanna says, and Logan shakes his head. "We bought him a carpet with a spaceship on it, and we bought him a telescope, so he can see the stars." He just nods.

"We bought stuff for sissy also," he says of his sister. "Mommy, is sissy going to poop in her pants?" he asks me, and Hunter answers.

"Yup, just like you did." Hunter leans in and kisses his neck while he giggles.

"Are you guys ready to go?" Dominic asks. "The new owners said for you guys to get the f-" he almost said fuck but stopped when he looked at Hunter, "to get out so they can get in."

"Rachel would never tell me to get out of my own home," Hunter says.

"It's not our house anymore," I tell him. "Let's go. I'm tired, and I need to put my feet up, and now I'm craving ice cream."

We walk out of the house, looking back one more time, and smile at each other.

That night when I walk into our new house, I smile as I look around my dream home. Directly on the beach like the other one but with five more bedrooms. I walk through the house that has already been unpacked, thanks to all of our friends and family members. I grab a water bottle and head upstairs, going straight to Logan's room. I stand at the doorway and watch my husband read him a bedtime story. Logan's trying to fight sleep, but he's losing the battle. I drink the water, watching them, and Hunter finishes the whole story even knowing that Logan has long ago fallen asleep. He kisses him on the forehead and turns off the light before coming to me.

"Are you okay?" he asks me, and I just smile at him as he takes my hand, and we walk to our bedroom.

The picture of us on the beach with me in his arms the night he proposed to me hangs right over our headboard. That was the first picture we hung up when we got into the house, and then we added other pictures next to it. Our wedding day, then the first ultrasound picture. My eyes go to the next picture; it's our first family picture. Logan's placed on my chest, my eyes on him as I cry in joy, and Hunter looking at both of us as he shed his own tears. Two more pictures are hanging there. One is of the ultrasound picture of our baby girl and other is an empty frame for a picture waiting to be added.

One month later, I place the picture in the frame, and it's almost identical to Logan's except Logan is in Hunter's arms as he points at his sister, Corina Joanna.

I hang the picture and look at the wall. Who would have known that being set up on that blind date would have gotten me mixed up in love?

The End

BOOKS BY NATASHA MADISON

Something Series
Something So Right
Something So Perfect
Something So Irresistible
Something So Unscripted

Tempt Series
Tempt The Boss
Tempt The Playboy
Tempt The Neighbor

Heaven & Hell Series
Hell and Back
Pieces of Heaven
Heaven & Hell Box Set
Love Series
Perfect Love Story
Unexpected Love Story
Broken Love Story

ACKNOWLEDGMENTS

My Husband: Thank you for being by my side through this whole thing.

My Kids: Matteo, Michael, and Erica, thank you for letting me do this. Thank you for being proud of me, I love you honey bunches and oats!

Rachel: You are my blurb bitch. Each time you do it without even reading this book and you rocked it. I'm so happy that I didn't give up when you ignored my many messages.

Dani: You are hands down one of the most genuine person I've ever met thank you so much for guiding me.

Lori: I don't know what I would do without you in my life. You take over and I don't even have to ask or worry because I know everything will be fine, because you're a rock star, I'm also scared of that whip!

Beta girls: Teressa, Natasha M, Lori, Sandy, Yolanda, Yamina. For three weeks I bombarded your messages with chapters and you ate it up. Thank you for holding my hand, telling me when things sucked and for being by my side.

Madison Maniacs: This little group went from two people to so much more and I can't thank you guys enough. This group is my go to, my safe place. You push me and get excited for me and I can't wait to watch us grow even bigger!

Julie: Thank you for taking my book with all its mistakes and making it pretty, or as pretty as it can be.

BLOGGERS. THANK YOU FOR TAKING A CHANCE ON ME. You give so much of yourself effortlessly and you are the voice that we can't do this without.

And Lastly and most importantly to YOU the reader, without you none of this would be real. So thank you for reading!

Made in the USA
Middletown, DE
08 March 2022